"Maybe you've been hurt deeply in life—even as a child. Maybe you've been misunderstood and rejected. Maybe you feel that your parents really don't want you around. I know what that's like. I've been there."

Outwardly, she was tough and defiant—right up to the minute a cell door closed behind her. Then she discovered the real Vicki Hensley—frustrated, fearful, and in desperate need of love. Find out how a prison sentence actually opened the door to freedom for a hardened young woman. And find out how her dramatic story can make a difference in *your* life, wherever you happen to be right now.

BY John Benton

Carmen
Teenage Runaway
Crazy Mary
Cindy
Patti
Suzie
Marji
Lori
Sherrie
Marji and the Kidnap Plot
Julie
Debbie
Lefty
Vicki

VICKI

JOHN BENTON

NEW HOPE
BOOKS

Fleming H. Revell Company
Old Tappan, New Jersey

Scripture quotations are from the King James Version of the Bible.

ISBN: 0-8007-8402-2
A New Hope Book
Copyright © 1981 by John Benton
All rights reserved
Printed in the United States of America

This is an original New Hope Book, published by New Hope Books, a Division of Fleming H. Revell Company, Old Tappan, New Jersey.

1

"For crying out loud, Vicki, put that gun away before somebody gets hurt!"

"I'm not kidding, Cecelia!" I said it as seriously as I knew how. "You give me all that money, or I'm going to pull this trigger, and you'll be deader than a doornail!"

Cecelia just shrugged and walked away from me toward the end of the bar. How was I going to convince her I was serious about robbing old man Gross's bar? Sure, Cecelia was my best friend; but I needed money for drugs, and I wasn't about to let anybody stand in my way. Besides, this was a perfect time. No one else was in the bar.

Even when I raised the pistol to eye level and aimed it right at her head, she still ignored me and began washing glasses.

So I cocked the gun and yelled, "Say your prayers, Cecelia, because I'm not fooling."

She kept on washing glasses.

"I'm counting to ten, Cecelia."

She kept washing.

"One, two, three . . ."

She threw a towel down in disgust and turned toward me. "Come on, Vicki. I know you're high. Besides, if you pull that trigger, you'll miss me by ten miles. You don't know how to handle a gun."

Well, that infuriated me. "Don't you dare insult me like that!" I shouted. "This is a .357 magnum I've got here.

Bought it off some dude on the street, and I've been practicing with it. I'm a dead shot, and that's what you're going to be—dead—if you don't do what I say. Now give me the money out of the cash register."

"Ha!" Cecelia laughed derisively. She pulled a glass out of the sink and held it high over her head. "Okay, if you're such a sharpshooter, let's see you break this glass. Then I'll listen."

She had called my bluff, so I carefully aimed at the glass and squeezed the trigger. The noise was deafening, and involuntarily I closed my eyes. And when I looked for the glass, Cecelia still held it high.

"See what I mean?" she said, laughing. "You couldn't hit the broad side of a barn."

That made me all the madder. "Hold that glass up again!" I ordered. "This time I won't miss!"

Still laughing, she returned the glass to its position high above her head.

I aimed carefully, steadying my hand as best I could. I had to get this one if I was going to carry this thing out. Once again I squeezed the trigger. Again the roar was deafening. But this time, crack! Glass splattered everywhere!

Shaken, Cecelia marched over to where I stood. "Okay, Vicki, this has gone far enough. You take you and your gun and hightail it out that door before I call the cops!"

Pointing the gun right at her head, I said, "Cecelia, you know I'm high. I do crazy things when I'm high. But since you're my friend, I'm going to take it easy on you. All I'm asking you to do now is to turn around and march into that back room and mind your own business. I'm going to go over and take all the money out of the cash register. You're going to pretend you don't know who did it or what happened, just that someone came in and took the money while you were in the back room. Do you understand what I'm saying?"

"Vicki, get some sense in your head," she pleaded. "I know you're high. I know you need money for drugs. But this is no way for you to do it. I'm your friend. Think about it. Suppose you do rob me. You know what's going to happen next? The cops are going to come and ask who did it. How am I going to tell them that my best friend did it? They won't buy that story about my being in the back room. So are you trying to say that you want me to rat on you, Vicki? You're putting me under terrible pressure. Besides, you used to work here. Former employees are always at the top of the list of suspects. Mr. Gross knows you're on drugs."

With that she wheeled around and started toward the end of the bar to wash more glasses.

"Stop right there, Cecelia!" I screamed. "Don't you dare take one more step! Friend or no friend, I'll drop you in your tracks if you don't do what I say!"

As she turned to face me, I said, "I'm getting terribly nervous and frustrated. I've got to pull this off quick."

"Mr. Gross will be walking in that door any minute now," she said. "If he sees you with that gun, it's going to be all over for you, Vicki."

Laughing, I replied, "I took care of old man Gross. He's over at Methodist Hospital. It'll take him at least half an hour to get there and another half an hour to get back. Let's see." I glanced at my watch. "I've still got forty-five minutes."

"Whatever are you talking about?"

"You know that phone call he got about fifteen minutes ago?"

Cecelia nodded.

"Well, I disguised my voice and told him his sister had been injured in an accident and he was needed at the hospital immediately."

"You didn't!" Cecelia exploded. "That poor man probably went ninety miles an hour to get to his sister. I'm telling you, when he finds out you did that, Vicki, he's going to kill you! Vicki, Vicki, don't you remember a few months ago when you were dead broke—no job, no nothing—and Mr. Gross hired you? He really did you a big favor, you know."

"Listen, Cecelia, I earned that money. I tantalized the men and got them to drink more. If you ask me, I was the one doing old man Gross a favor."

"Maybe, but he did you a bigger favor. Four times I remember your coming to work stoned out of your mind. He kept warning you. But no—you wouldn't listen. No wonder he finally had to can you. And now you try to pull something like this. Stupid!"

"You're brainwashed," I replied. "Haven't you seen the terrible things booze does to people? You know what it did to my own mother. It ruins homes; it ruins lives; it takes money that ought to be spent for food and milk for little children. But you, Cecelia, and that dirty, filthy, old man Gross, you keep selling the stuff to these people. Don't you have any guilt over that?"

She just stared at me. I knew I had her. So I decided to keep the argument in that vein. "And that's why I'm here. I'm going to get even with old man Gross for the dirty deeds he is doing in this neighborhood."

"Oh, come on, Vicki," she said in disgust. "Anybody who's a junkie like you has got no room to criticize someone who sells a little booze."

"Okay," I yelled, "this conversation has gone far enough. Time is running out. So you walk back there, and don't be watching me. That way you can tell the cops some-body stole the money while you were in the back room."

"Vicki, please let me talk some sense into your head. No way is this going to work. You won't get by with it."

"Cecelia, get back there right now!" I screamed. "There is no way you are going to talk me out of this. I need money for drugs. I don't want to shoot you and leave your little kids as orphans, but I will do it if I have to!"

I don't know if it was the mention of her kids that changed her mind, but much to my surprise she turned and walked into the back room without another protest. I dashed around the end of the bar and headed for the cash register.

I knew exactly how it worked, so when I pushed the right button, it flew open—almost so fast that it startled me. I scooped up the bills, thinking that business must have been brisk this evening—there was a lot of money in there.

As I was stuffing the money into my purse, the front door opened. Oh, no! How did old man Gross get back so soon? Now I'd had it! I could see those prison bars already.

I spun around, the gun still in my hand. If it was Gross, I was going to pull the trigger. No way were they going to bust me!

"Hey, lady," a man's voice boomed out, "what in the world is this? Don't point that gun at me!"

Hank Quattaro! He was one of the regulars here. I had served him many times.

"Oh, Hank, am I glad it's you," I said. "I just got a crazy telephone call from some guy who said he was coming to rob us. So I went and got Mr. Gross's gun to be ready for him. Say, that wasn't you who called, was it?"

Laughing, Hank said, "Yeah, that was me. I confess. But I wasn't coming down to rob your money. I was coming down to get you, Vicki. Don't you know you're my favorite girl?"

"Hank, be serious," I countered. "I am absolutely scared to death. And I sure am glad to see you. If that guy comes in now, he's not as likely to try something with you here."

Hank staggered up to the bar and plunked himself on a stool. I guess he was drunk, as usual. "Since you're here protecting me, I'll give you a free beer," I told him. I knew that would keep him busy for a few minutes. I wanted to get back to that back room where Cecelia was. Old man Gross kept more of his money back there.

As I grabbed the glass and poured Hank his favorite brew, I remembered another problem. Hank knew I had been here. He would be a witness when the police came—and that would point the finger of suspicion right at me—even if Cecelia told them what I told her to tell them.

As I walked to the end of the bar, I noticed Hank looking me up and down. That dirty old man. But that gave me an idea. I grabbed my purse and walked over next to where he was sitting. Before he knew what was going on, I threw my arms around him and hugged him tight. I began to rub my hands down his back, and he started to respond.

"Wow!" he exclaimed. "This is my lucky night. Free beer. And now this. The service in this place has really picked up!"

I giggled, and so did he. Then I puckered my lips. His eyes grew wide, and he threw out his arms. "Kiss me, baby!" he shouted. "Kiss me!"

I held my breath—because he stunk so. But I pressed my lips against his as he threw his arms around me.

While I had him sidetracked, I reached into my purse, grabbed a few bills, and stuffed them into Hank's coat pocket. He didn't feel a thing because his mind was else-where at that moment.

I gently pulled myself away to arm's length. "Goodness, Vicki," he said, almost drooling. "Why don't we run off and get married now? I mean, that was absolutely fantas-tic!"

He reached toward me, but I backed off and headed to-ward the back room. I guess Hank knew that was all he was going to get, for he rather meekly returned to his beer.

Cecelia was waiting there in the back room. "Now aren't you smart?" she said in disgust. "I was listening to every-thing that was going on. Now what are you going to do?"

"You never mind," I countered. "Just turn and look to-ward that wall. I know old man Gross keeps money hidden in the bottom drawer of his desk. I have seen that old cigar box many times. And while I am taking that, you just look the other way. Remember, you didn't see a thing."

"Vicki, you're crazy. Why don't you just hand over the money you've taken from the cash register and get out of here while you can? You know this is going to be big trou-ble for you."

"Cecelia, it'll be bigger trouble for you if you don't do as I say. Now face that wall." I motioned with my gun.

She reluctantly obeyed. I ran over to the desk, pulled out the bottom drawer, and searched a few moments until I found the cigar box—full of money. This guy was really stupid.

I grabbed that money, stuffed it into my purse, put the box back in its usual place, shut the desk, and said, "Okay, Cecelia, turn around and look right at me. Now get this straight."

She turned, arms folded, looking defiant.

"I'm getting out of here now. When I do, you go back to the cash register and open it. Then you scream, 'Somebody robbed me!' Hank will stand there looking at you, and you will call the cops. When the cops come, you tell them that some bills are missing from the cash register. You tell them you were in the back room while Hank was out here by himself. Suggest that the cops check Hank. They'll find some bills in his right coat pocket."

"What?" Cecelia asked in shocked horror. "You're not going to put the weight on Hank, are you?"

"You don't expect me to carry the weight, do you?" I sneered. "You just do what I say, and let the cops figure out what they want to do next. Of course Hank will scream he's innocent. But as the cops are always saying, that'll be up to the judge. Hank's too drunk to know what's going on, anyway."

"Vicki, I never thought I'd see you stoop so low!" Cecelia declared. "You won't get by with it."

"Don't you worry," I told her. "All you have to do is remember you didn't see a thing. You came back here, and when you went back to the bar, the money was gone. You didn't see anyone back here. And if Hank says anything about seeing me, you just say he must be having another of his delusions."

As I headed for the back door, I glanced around. Cecelia still hadn't moved. But I was hoping she was too good a friend to rat on me. At least I had the money.

The streetlight on the corner gave an eerie glow to the alley. Nervously I walked two blocks and hailed the first cab I saw. I guess I had reason to be nervous. I must have had over two thousand dollars in my purse! Not a bad haul!

I told the driver to take me to Bourbon Street. Here in New Orleans, that was a great place to buy drugs. My connection, Leon Prout, was usually around Bourbon Street, and Leon always seemed to have a good supply of Dilaudids—and they were my heaven.

I hurried inside a bar where I usually could find Leon. Sure enough, there he was. But when I asked him for forty tablets, he looked at me in surprise. "Forty? You know that'll be sixteen hundred bucks?"

Laughing, I responded, "Of course I know that. What's the matter? Don't you know you're dealing with a big-time girl?" I leaned toward him and opened my purse. "Look here." He could see all the money crammed in and my gun sitting on top of it all.

One look and he jerked back in surprise. "Vicki, what did you do? Stick up a bank?"

"Yeah, First National," I said with a laugh. "I walked into their big vault, and there were buckets of money all over the place. But I wasn't selfish. I took only a little bit so they can still open for business tomorrow."

Leon knew I was putting him on, but he carried the story along anyway. "That's sure nice of you, Vicki. I can't stand these slobs who take everything for themselves and don't leave anything for the poor. You are indeed a good girl."

We both had a good laugh at our cleverness. I knew Leon didn't care where I got the money—just so I had it.

"I don't carry forty tablets on me," Leon said, "so come on over to my apartment. I've got them there."

We walked a few blocks to a large apartment house still in the French Quarter. His apartment had real class.

I settled into a comfortable chair while he went into his bedroom. Moments later he came out with a large bag and counted out forty tablets on the coffee table. "Okay, that'll be sixteen hundred dollars."

I reached into my purse and began pulling out money,

straightening it out, and counting. When I got to sixteen hundred dollars, I handed it to him.

Leon recounted. "Hey, wait a minute!" he exclaimed. "There's only fifteen hundred dollars here. You trying to cheat me?"

He counted the money right in front of me, and, sure enough, it was one hundred dollars short. So I counted out another one hundred dollars and gave it to him, all the while protesting it was an honest mistake.

When he pushed the tablets over toward me, I started counting. "Hey, there's only thirty-eight here," I said. "Now who's cheating?"

"Vicki, I never cheat," Leon said soberly. "I may be a pusher, but I'm an honest pusher."

We recounted the tablets, and sure enough there were forty of them there. I mumbled something about how anybody can make a mistake and that it was a rough night.

And Leon, an honest pusher? The whole idea made me laugh. Could anybody trust anybody else in the drug world? Right now I was worried about Cecelia. Could I trust her to keep her mouth shut? Or would she rat on me?

As I stood to leave, Leon said, "Vicki, when your money runs out, I've got a great thing going. I sure could use someone like you to help me. So let me know when you need some money."

I stiffened. "Listen, Leon, I wasn't born yesterday. I want you to get something straight. I'm no prostitute—and never will be!"

He threw his head back and guffawed. "Vicki, Vicki, quit jumping to conclusions. I'm no pimp."

Many of my friends had gone out on the streets prostituting; they all had their pimps who lived off their earnings.

And the way Leon was looking at me, I was sure that was what he had in mind.

"Come on, Leon," I said, "I know what you're up to. You can get your filthy eyes off me. I'm not that kind of girl."

"Wait a minute, Vicki. Like I told you, I'm no pimp. I've just got something going, and I need a girl like you to help me."

Even the word *prostitute* repulsed me. I'd made up my mind that that was one thing I'd never do.

"What do you have in mind, then?" I questioned.

"Not now. When you run out of money, then you come and see me and we'll talk about it. This thing is too good to be true, so I'm not telling anyone. But when you're out of money and need more drugs, you come and see me. I think we would do well in this partnership."

"Partnership?"

"Not now, Vicki. Like I say, come and see me when you need the money. Then I'll give you the details."

The mystery of it intrigued me, but I really didn't want to have to depend on someone else. I was going to make it on my own. So I said, "I'll never need you, Leon." I patted my purse. "Just me and my gun walking through life together—we're great partners. And that will always bring me enough money."

"Don't be so positive, Vicki. Sometimes things get hot, and you've got to lay low. That's when you can come and see me. I mean, I've got a great deal for you."

As I headed for the door, I called back, "I'll see you again, Leon, when I need some more drugs. But I'll always have my own money. Sorry."

He laughed. "It'll get hot for you. Remember that!"

I wasn't too worried about getting home late because my grandmother was out of town for several days and I had the place to myself. But I was in a hurry to get back because I wanted to get high.

Once there I got out my needle, took a Dilaudid, put it in the cooker, and shot up. It felt so good. I remember thinking that Leon somehow always managed to have good Dilaudids. . . .

The following evening when I answered the telephone, Cecelia's voice brought me back to reality: "Vicki," she said, "we are in serious trouble; I mean, real trouble."

"You didn't squeal on me, did you?"

"No, I didn't. But the police sure didn't believe that story about Hank. I told you they wouldn't."

"Didn't you tell them to frisk him?"

"Yeah, and they did and found the bills you planted there. But Hank denied the whole story and said you were there. Well, the police dusted the cash register. You are really stupid, Vicki. If Hank had robbed the cash register, his fingerprints would have been all over it. But you know as well as I do that the only prints they're going to find are mine and Mr. Gross's." She paused to be sure the next two words would sink in: "And yours!"

She was right. I was stupid. Why didn't I think of the fingerprint angle? I could have worn gloves. But I still knew her testimony against me would be the most damaging.

"Cecelia, you didn't see who robbed the bar, did you?"

There was a long pause. Then the receiver clicked.

Well, that made me furious—and a little frightened. I immediately dialed her number, and the phone rang and rang. Finally she answered it.

"Listen, Cecelia, don't you hang up on me again!" I screamed. "That's no way to treat a friend. Now you'd better keep that story straight. You saw nothing. And I mean, nothing!"

I kept ranting about it, but she didn't respond.

When I got through, I waited. Finally she said, "Vickie, I don't know how long I can cover for you. The cops have been here all day. They've threatened me; they're putting me under a lot of pressure. They even told me if I didn't tell the truth, they were going to take away my kids!"

"What do you mean, take away your kids?" I yelled. "You know there's no way they can do that just because they think you are withholding information."

"They said they would, Vicki. They said they would arrest me for this robbery because I would be a logical suspect—that I stole the money and then said it was a robbery. It's happened before. Well, if they arrest me, they said they would have to find a place for my kids. The court would send them to some foster home, and I would have no control whatsoever over where my kids went. And they said they would send me away for years."

"Cecelia, they are just trying to scare you," I interrupted. "They don't really mean all that."

"I wouldn't be so sure, Vicki. Besides, I couldn't stand it if they sent my kids off to some unknown place. I couldn't take that!"

Now I was really worried. They had found Cecelia's weak spot, and they were playing it for all they were worth.

"What are you trying to tell me, Cecelia? Are you trying to say that if they bust you, you'll rat on me?"

The silence seemed interminable. Finally she said, "Vicki, if I were you, I'd get out of town fast. I'd head for Mexico. Because if they lay a hand on my kids, I'm going to tell the truth. You may be my friend, but my kids mean more to me than your friendship. If they touch my kids, I'm going to have to tell them. So get out of town now while you've got a chance!"

Again the telephone clicked. But this time I just sat there with the receiver in my hand, stunned. I sure didn't feel like calling her back. After all, what good would it do? She had made it clear that if it were a choice between me and her kids, I didn't stand a chance!

What was I going to do? Should I head for Mexico? I needed time to think. But what would happen if the cops came looking for me right now?

I jumped up and bolted every door. If they came now, would I have a shoot-out with them? Or should I run before they got here? How close were they to cracking the case? How much time did I have to decide?

2

I always felt more secure when Grandma was home—and she should be back soon. My real mother lived across town, but my Grandmother had raised me, and I lived with her. I was illegitimate, and my mom was embarrassed to have me around. I guess when I was younger, I also inhibited her rather freewheeling life-style.

In some ways it seemed like my real mom was more like a sister to me and like Grandmother was my mother. I knew Grandma really loved me. But I had also discovered her major weakness: I could talk her out of almost anything.

When she did return from her trip, I was high. She took one look at me and said that I looked sleepy. Poor Grandma. She didn't know the difference between someone's being high and sleepy.

"It's okay; I'm resting," I told her. I just sat there nodding in the big chair in the living room. Those Dilaudids were safe. Some of my friends took heroin, but you had to be careful messing around with that stuff here in New Orleans. Some of the biggest rip-off agents in the country congregated here. And they wouldn't think twice about selling you rat poison instead of heroin! Every so often I would read in the newspapers about someone dying from an overdose. I knew better. It was no drug overdose; it was rat poison that had been sold to some unsuspecting junkie as heroin!

I didn't worry about the Dilaudids that way. The companies that made them were inspected by the government. So when you bought a Dilaudid, you didn't have to worry about rat poison. But at forty dollars a tablet, they were expensive!

Grandma's voice brought me out of my reverie. "Vicki, you almost fell out of that chair! What's the matter? Have you been staying up all night and chasing boys while I was gone?"

"Now, Grandma," I laughed, "how do I know what you've been doing for the past few days? You told me you were going to visit relatives. But I'll bet you've been down on Bourbon Street shacked up with some young dude!"

She returned my laughter and said wistfully, "How I wish!"

"Grandma, maybe we can work out a deal. You get me an old man with lots of money, and I'll get you a young, handsome guy. How's that for a deal?"

She just smiled. Fortunately for me she did have quite a sense of humor, and I had learned how to use it when she got on my case.

She headed to the kitchen for a cup of coffee and then came and sat on the sofa facing me. I said something about a cup of coffee sounding good, and she went and got me one, too. Then we both just sat there sipping coffee and not saying anything. But I knew she had something on her mind.

She acted like she was trying to find the words to say it. Then, in all seriousness, she asked, "Vicki, are you high?"

I had a mouthful of coffee at that instant, and I spit it out all over me and the chair as I almost choked. Some spilled from the cup onto my lap, too.

Jumping to my feet I screamed, "High? What in the world are you talking about, Grandma?" I brushed the coffee off my clothes and the chair, took my cup, and headed for the kitchen mumbling, "I'd better get me another cup."

Grandma didn't say a word or try to follow up her obvious advantage. But I could sense her eyes following me as I stumbled into the kitchen. I grabbed the coffeepot and poured. Rats! I missed the cup. So I tried again. This time I got more inside the cup than outside. I also grabbed a rag and wiped up the mess I had made on the cabinet and the floor.

I put milk and sugar into the coffee and walked carefully into the living room. No way was I going to stagger now, and I opened my eyes as wide as I could. I had to keep Grandma fooled.

As I eased into the big chair, Grandma was still watching me. "I'm surprised at you," I told her. "What makes you think I'm high?"

She leaned forward and began, a note of sadness in her voice, "Vicki, it was impossible not to see what just happened. You had trouble walking straight when you went into the kitchen. I saw you pour coffee and miss the cup. And when you did come back in here, your hand was shaking like I don't know what. Take a look at your saucer; it's full of coffee."

I glanced down. Sure enough, the coffee was almost overflowing the saucer. How come I hadn't noticed that before?

"Grandma, Grandma, don't tell me you haven't had days when you've poured coffee and missed the cup. Come on, be reasonable. You can trust me—I'm not high."

She leaned back and sipped her coffee. But her eyes seemed to be boring into me, revealing my true self. I couldn't take it.

"Quit staring at me!"

"I was just checking your eyes, Vicki," she answered quietly. "You can say all you want, but your eyes keep closing halfway. I read somewhere that that's a sign a person is high."

"Oh, Grandma, come off it!" I exploded. "You read one article and all of a sudden you are an expert on drug addicts. Boy, it sure is true that a little knowledge is a dangerous thing!"

"You'd better go to bed and sleep it off," she counseled.

"I'm not going to bed!" I yelled. "I'm going to stay up and watch TV, and I'll stay up all night if I want to. I'm not a little baby anymore!"

I really didn't want to go to bed because I didn't want to fall asleep and lose this high. It felt too good.

I kept nodding. Finally she came over, grabbed me by the arm, and pulled me up. "Come on, little girl, into bed now," she said.

Should I resist her? I really felt like belting her, but I didn't want to foul up my high. So I decided it would be easier to go along. I didn't have to go to sleep even if I went to bed, I told myself.

"Okay, okay, have it your way," I said, and headed for my bedroom. I shut the door behind me, sat on the edge of the bed, and began to scratch my nose. The sensations were so overwhelming that I just sort of leaned over and drifted into my beautiful dream world.

Suddenly my bedroom door flew open. Through a haze I saw someone towering over me. "Vicki, what are these things?" a voice screamed.

I focused on the outstretched hand that was almost touching my nose. Oh, no! My works! Where in the world did she get them? I abruptly sat up and realized Grandma was ranting and raving about something.

"I found these in the bathroom!" I heard her say.

How stupid of me. I forgot to hide my works after I got off the last time. I guess I hadn't expected her back so soon. And I was high when she came in, so I didn't even think of them. How could I be so careless? What's more, how was I going to get out of this one? She had the goods!

"Okay, Grandma, I'll level with you. I really hated to tell you this because I know how you worry about me. But last night I got real scared here by myself. I thought I heard someone trying to get in. Foolishly I had told several people you were gone, so I was afraid some weirdo knew I was here alone. I had just about decided to call the cops. But then I thought of my friend Van Monoleff."

"You called whom?" she interrupted.

I had made up that name, so I had to think quickly. "Van's a real nice kid," I said. "His dad's a police officer. You see, I thought that if I called the police, they might not take it seriously. Besides, there're some cops I wouldn't feel safe inviting in in the middle of the night! So I decided to call Van. At least he would take me seriously. And we'd be close to the police if we needed them; I knew his dad would listen to him."

"That's all very well, young lady, but what about these?" She pushed the works toward me again.

"I was getting to that. You see, I thought Van was such a nice boy, such a good boy. Well, he came over, and, you know, he didn't try anything. You know what I mean, don't you?"

She smiled faintly and said, "You mean sex?"

"Yeah, Grandma, that's what I mean. He didn't try anything like that. But I couldn't believe what that guy did. He said he had to go to the bathroom and excused himself. Well, he was in there such a long time that I started to get worried. I was scared to death that he would come out stark naked and try to rape me. But when he finally opened that door, he was fully clothed. But, and you may not believe this, Grandma, he was higher than a kite. I couldn't believe it myself—a police officer's son on drugs! Well, as soon as I saw what was going on, I knew I had to get him out of the house. I knew that if you came in and found him here high, you'd really throw a fit—maybe even throw me out, too. Besides, if someone really was trying to break in and I had to call the cops, how would I explain Van's condition? I was really in a fix, so I threw him out."

She stood there staring at me. Was my story working?

"Grandma, evidently he left his set of works in the bathroom. That's what you've got there. I wouldn't even know how to use that needle and whatever that other stuff is there. I know nothing about those kind of things."

Should I keep talking? Did she believe me? I didn't have long to wait, for she raised those works high over her head, slammed them onto the floor, and jumped up and down on the broken pieces, screaming, "May these works be sent to the pit of hell. And may that young man be found out and go to jail for desecrating my house!"

Wow! Rarely had I seen that side of Grandma! She usually was tolerant and rather easygoing. But she sure was against drugs! Well, at least my story had worked. Sure, she had broken my works, and I didn't have another set. But I could worry about that tomorrow.

Grandma wheeled, slammed the door after her, and

stomped down the hall. Emotionally exhausted, I fell back into bed. That was close. Almost too close!

When I awoke, I stretched and looked at the clock. Already eleven! I got up, dressed, and headed to the kitchen for some coffee. Grandma was sitting in the living room with her ever-present cup.

I poured my cup, hitting it dead center this time. I checked to be sure I didn't have any in the saucer. Then I headed for the big chair in the living room. But I didn't have to worry about Grandma watching me. She was sitting there staring out into space, apparently oblivious to my presence. Then I looked closely and noticed the tears trickling down her cheeks. What had happened?

"Grandma," I said as tenderly as I could, "what's the matter?"

She just shook her head.

I set my coffee down on a table, sat next to her on the sofa, and slipped my arm around her. "Grandma, has something happened to my mother?"

She started sobbing, and I hugged her tight. "Grandma, you can tell me. I'm an adult now. I can handle things. You've always loved me and cared for me; and I feel the same about you. Whatever it is, you can tell me."

She turned to face me. "Vicki, the police were here earlier this morning."

I dropped my arm like I was shot and jumped up. "The police? What in the world were the police doing here?"

She didn't answer. She didn't have to. I figured they had pressured Cecelia into ratting on me. But did the police tell Grandma why they were looking for me? How much did she know?

"What did they want?" I asked.

"Well, they didn't say. They just wanted to know where you were the other night. Now, Vicki, I don't know what you've been up to, but I had to do something I've never done before for you. I lied to those policemen. I told them you had gone with me for two days to visit my oldest son and his wife in Little Rock, Arkansas. Vicki, I knew that younger policeman; he was Frances Billings's boy. I just hated to lie to that young man, but I had to cover for you."

What was I going to say? Grandma had saved my skin, and I loved her for that. But could I level with her?

"I think we should have a grandmother-granddaughter talk," she went on. "If you have been up to something wrong, you had better tell me. Those policemen said they would be in touch with me. I told them you were at some girl friend's house now and would be back this afternoon. So they are coming by here again at three. And you'd better start telling me the truth right now!"

I figured there was only one thing to do: plead ignorance.

"Grandma," I said, "I don't have the slightest idea what those cops want. In fact, I think I'll just run down to the station right now and get this all cleared up. Or I'll wait here until three if you think that would be best. I'll be more than happy to talk to any cops. I have done absolutely nothing wrong."

"Vicki, there was some talk of a robbery," Grandma said. "You haven't been out robbing, have you?" She moved uneasily on the sofa.

Well, I guess I didn't have to wonder now whether or not Cecelia had ratted on me.

"Grandma, how can you talk about me that way?" I protested. "You brought me up to be honest. I don't know anything about any robbery. Believe me, Grandma, I've been a good girl while you were away."

She slowly edged onto one hip, reached under the other hip, and pulled something out. I couldn't believe my eyes. She had my .357 magnum in her hand!

I feigned a look of utter surprise and said, "What's that? What's that?"

"Vicki, Vicki, don't pull that innocent act on me. Please don't insult my intelligence. You know very well what this is."

"Of course, I know what it is," I replied. "It's a gun. And I'm scared to death of them."

She turned it over in her hand, and I screamed, "Put that thing down before it goes off and somebody gets hurt!"

"What's the matter, Vicki? Do you know it's loaded?" She didn't wait for me to answer as she continued, "I don't know what I'm going to do with you. I don't know whether to spank you, beat you, throw you out of my house, or call the cops. Now you know all about this gun, so why don't you start telling me the truth?"

"Grandma, I am telling you the truth. I don't know a thing about that gun!"

"Oh, yes, you do!" Grandma shouted. "You see, while you were asleep, I went into your bedroom and looked into your purse. I found a lot of money in there. And I found this gun. You know this is your gun, Vicki. Admit it!"

Now what was I going to say? She had me cold! Stalling, I walked to the window and looked out, not really seeing anything, but thinking hard.

"Okay, Grandma, I didn't want to say anything because I was trying to cover for my friend Van Monoleff. But you deserve an explanation. Remember I told you how he came out of the bathroom high? Well, I pushed him out the front door. But as I pushed him out, that gun you're holding fell from his coat pocket. I started to give it back to him, but I worried about how he was acting—and he wasn't very happy about my making him leave. I didn't know what to do. If I handed him the gun, he might even turn it on me. You know, then he could have raped me at gunpoint or even killed me. There's no telling what he'd do when he was high like that. So I decided I'd just keep his gun for a day or two. I didn't know anywhere to hide it, so I stuck it in my purse. I didn't think you'd stoop so low as to be a purse snooper, and. . . ."

Before she knew what was happening, I had wheeled around, stomped over to her, and grabbed the gun out of her hand.

"Vicki! Vicki! What are you doing? You give that gun back to me!"

I wasn't going to put up with any more of her interrogation. Besides, if the police were coming, I knew I had to get away.

"I've had it! I've had it!" I yelled. "I'm sick and tired of trying to cover up for Van. I'm taking this gun right down to the police station. Furthermore, I'm going to face those two cops who came here and tell them to stop accusing me of robberies. . . ."

By this time I had stomped into my bedroom, stuffed the gun into my purse, grabbed a raincoat, and headed back through the living room for the front door. "Okay, Grandma, I'm going to get this thing cleared up. I'll be back in a little while."

The whole house rattled as I slammed the door after me. I hit the front steps on the run. I didn't know for sure where I was going, but I had my purse, my money, my gun, and my—oh, no! I had forgotten my Dilaudids! I couldn't leave them behind!

I wheeled around and marched into the house, not even

bothering to shut the front door after me. Grandma was still sitting on the sofa staring into space. "Forgot my driver's license," I explained, "in case they need some identification."

Heading for my bedroom, I slammed the door behind me. I always hid my drugs in a little slit in the mattress, so I jerked back the covers, grabbed the package, and stuffed it into my bra.

Out of my bedroom, down the hall, and through the living room I stomped, yelling, "Good-bye, Grandma. And you had better pray for those cops. Right now I feel like busting them in the nose for falsely accusing me!"

"If you were just going after your driver's license," she said softly, "why did you slam the bedroom door shut? Were you trying to hide something from me?"

I was right at the door, ready to go out. But that remark made me explode inside. I wheeled around and yelled, "Grandma, will you quit treating me like a baby? I'm over twenty-one. Don't you know what you've raised?"

She stared at me, her mouth open, lips quivering.

"Grandma, you've raised a dirty, filthy junkie! I'm hooked, and hooked good! Take a look here!"

I reached into my blouse and pulled out the package of Dilaudids. "See these? They are my master now, Grandma! These drugs! I'm a junkie! And yes, Grandma, the cops are after me. I did rob; I did steal!"

I stuffed the Dilaudids back into my bra. Then I rolled up my sleeve and shouted, "Grandma, take a look at this. That's where I plunge the needle in." I pointed. "I plunge and plunge and plunge! I'm hooked, Grandma! I've got to have my drugs!"

I was standing right in front of her by that time. She put out her arms toward me. I just pushed them aside and continued yelling, "I'm a girl without hope, Grandma. I'm hooked, and soon my miserable life will be over!"

"Vicki! Vicki!" she pleaded, tears coursing down her cheeks. "Don't go out that door! There *is* hope for you!"

I knew better, and I dashed outside before her tears got to me. I ran down the sidewalk and along the street as fast as I could. But where to now? I was mad at myself; I was mad at Grandma; I was mad at the cops; and I was especially mad at Cecelia. If I got a chance, I was going to kill her.

A couple of blocks from Grandma's I spotted a phone booth and dialed Cecelia's number.

When she answered, I screamed, "Cecelia, I want you to level with me. If you're not telling the truth, I'll come over there and kill your two kids and then blow your brains out!"

When she didn't respond, I knew I had her.

"Did you call the cops?" I demanded.

There was a long pause. Then *click!*

I couldn't stand her hanging up on me like that, so I dialed the number again. When she finally answered, I shouted, "Cecelia, let me get something to you straight. If you want to see those kids of yours stay alive, you are going to do exactly as I say. You hang up on me again, and I'll come over and get your kids! Now you had better start talking to me. Did you squeal to the cops?"

There was another long pause, and I screamed again, "Cecelia, you had better answer me right now, or I'm coming over. I'm giving you three seconds. Did you squeal to the cops?"

Still no answer. My blood boiled. Some friend she turned out to be! "Cecelia, answer me!" I screamed.

Infuriated, I was about to hang up myself and head for

her place. Then I heard a man's voice: "Vicki Hensley, this is Detective Kantor, New Orleans Police Department. I think it would be a good idea if you met me down at the station to discuss this matter."

I slammed the receiver down, jerked open the telephone booth door, and took off.

Cecelia *had* squealed. The cops were there with her now—and they were looking for *me*.

I sure couldn't go to Cecelia's. I couldn't go back to Grandma's. The cops would be there this afternoon. Besides, she wouldn't let me back in. I knew how she felt about drugs. And she sure wouldn't lie for me again.

I was running, but I didn't know where. Was there any place I could go? Did anybody care what happened to me?

3

I thought about taking a cab, but I knew they were too easy for the police to trace. So when I spotted a bus, I boarded it and headed for Bourbon Street. That was a good place to get lost in the crowd. There was always a lot of action there, and I could probably find someone to stay with.

When I got off the bus, I remembered what Leon had said about having a deal for me. I wasn't broke, but at least I could find out what he had in mind. Maybe it would amount to a place to stay.

He lived on Burgundy Street, so I started in that direction. But I didn't have to walk that far. He was on the street peddling drugs.

"Hey, Leon," I said as casually as I could, "what's up?"

He stared at me through his dark glasses. Then a smile filtered across his face. He knew I was coming his way.

"Vicki, darling," he said, "are you really ready to become a prostitute?"

I jerked back and snarled, "I thought we went through that last time, Leon. No way am I going to become a prostitute! You said you weren't a pimp."

"Naw," he said, laughing, "I'm no pimp. Those guys are the lowest of the low."

I was so delighted to have found Leon so readily that I hadn't noticed a burly guy leaning against a nearby building. But I sure noticed when this guy lunged forward, socking Leon squarely in the jaw with his fist.

The blow spun Leon around. I saw his eyes roll to the back of his head. His legs looked like jelly as he crumpled to the sidewalk. He didn't know what had hit him.

What on earth was going on? Should I stay put—or run? Well, if the guy had overheard our comments about prostitution and was after me, I was sure going to run!

But I guess I didn't have to worry, for the big guy acted like I wasn't even there. He straddled Leon's prostrate body and yelled, "Get up this minute, you filthy drug pusher. We'll settle this matter right now!"

Who was this guy? Had Leon dealt him some bad drugs? Poor Leon. It seemed that everybody—including the cops—had it in for the pushers.

Leon's eyes blinked several times as he started coming around. But when he rolled over to try to get up, the big guy hauled off and kicked him in the ribs just as hard as he could. Leon screamed, doubling up in agony.

When the guy kicked again, I had had it. I ran over and grabbed him, yelling, "Come on, man; you think you're some kind of macho man—kicking a guy when he's down? This guy didn't do anything—"

"What do you mean, he didn't do anything?" the big guy interrupted. "You heard what I just said!"

I tried to figure this guy out. Heavy gold chains around his neck set off his swanky suit. Big diamonds flashed on his four rings. He sure had money. He looked like—hey, that was it! The guy had to be a pimp! But why was he fighting with Leon?

Leon! His groans brought me back to the problem of the moment. I bent over him to try to help him. Then I felt the big guy's hand on my shoulder as he pulled me back up. "Come on, baby," he said, "you don't want to mess around with this filthy tramp. Come with me. I'll treat you right.

You can be a real woman with me."

I tried to jerk away, but by now he had me by both arms and was pushing me toward the curb. That's when I spotted the new white Cadillac in the NO PARKING zone. With its silver ornaments on the hood and chrome all over the sides, it had to be a pimp's car. Evidently he was rolling in money.

As I stiffened my legs to impede our progress toward the car, he said, "Hey, baby, stay cool! I mean, you and me will have a good time seeing the town. And, baby, I'll take good care of you. You'll be my own little dolly."

"Listen, mister," I protested, "I don't know who you are. But I think I know what you're up to, and I'm not that kind of girl."

He spun me around and looked right into my eyes. "Listen, baby, you've got it all wrong. I won't hurt you. I'm just going to take good care of you. I've got a nice little poodle dog I want to give you. And a fancy mink coat. I've got a beautiful apartment overlooking the river. And it's all yours—for free!"

I knew better. Nothing in life comes free. But I really didn't have much choice at the moment because he still had a firm grip on my arms. We were right beside the car, and he opened a door and started to push me inside.

Then I heard Leon scream, "Jimmy, stop right there! Don't you make one false move!"

Slowly, the guy released his grip on me and cautiously turned toward Leon, who still lay sprawled out on the sidewalk. But when I looked this time I saw that the balance had tilted. Leon had an arm extended and a pistol pointed right at the big guy.

"You lay a hand on that girl, and I'm pulling this trigger!" Leon yelled. "The last guy who tried to take away my girl ended up in the bottom of a bayou with a big hole in his head!"

So this was it—pimps fighting over girls. I knew they would kill each other to try to get girls for what they called their stables. But Leon was no pimp, was he? The other guy sure seemed to be. Was he about to pull a gun, too? Was I about to witness a shoot-out over me?

I edged away from the Cadillac, waiting for Leon to shoot or for Jimmy to grab me. But nothing happened. So I edged closer to Leon. I knew him. And maybe he wasn't a pimp.

Jimmy cautiously made his way to the driver's side, keeping a close eye on Leon the whole time. As he opened the door, he said, "Okay, Leon, you got the drop on me this time. But next time I belt you, I'll knock you out cold and then splatter your brains all over the sidewalk!"

Leon laughed derisively. "Listen, Jimmy, you're all talk. But the next time you come messing around, I might just pull this trigger first and ask questions later. Now get out of here!"

Ignoring him, Jimmy looked at me and called, "Baby, you are soon going to get tired of that small-time operator. A junkie—that's all he is. And, baby, when you get tired of him, just look me up. You'll never get tired of a real man like me!"

He flashed a huge smile. I must have looked like I was considering his offer, because Leon said, "Vicki, do you know who that big dude is? He's Jimmy Margo. His girls call him a slave master. Once you're in his stable, he'll kill you to keep you. Don't listen to him unless you want to live the life of a slave!"

Instead of getting into his car, Jimmy wheeled around and headed our way. Was he going to take me by force?

Leon kept the gun trained on him, but Jimmy acted as though he knew Leon wouldn't shoot. In fact, he walked right over and stood looking down at Leon. He spit on the sidewalk and yelled, "I don't take kindly to remarks like that! So I am going to tell you right to your face that I will come back and get you, Leon. You had better carry your gun where you can grab it quickly because I am going to sneak up on you and teach you a lesson that you'll never forget!"

Leon was still grimacing in pain, but he kept his gun trained on Jimmy's head. "I ought to blast that nose right off your dirty face!" he shouted. "Now get out of here quick before I do!"

Nothing happened. Jimmy just stood there. Would Leon shoot him? I guess they both had such big egos that neither of them would back down. A crowd was starting to gather, and in the distance I could see a couple of cops heading toward us.

Jimmy must have seen them, too, because he wheeled and got into his Cadillac. But as he did, he called to me, "Remember, baby, it won't be long until you find out what a creep this Leon is. I can offer you so much more!" He slammed the door, revved up the engine, and took off with the wheels squealing.

I helped Leon as he struggled to get up, holding his ribs in obvious pain. "I should have killed him, that's what I should have done," he muttered as we moved over to where he could lean up against the side of a building.

"Come on, now; is Jimmy really all that bad?"

"No," he replied. "I just had to let him know I wasn't

afraid of him. Besides, baby, you're more valuable to me than you are to him. I was just protecting my interest!"

He spotted the cops getting closer, so he motioned for me to help him walk away. He stuffed the gun in his pocket, safely out of sight, and hailed a nearby cab. "Cook's Funeral Home on Magnolia Street," he told the driver.

Now my curiosity really was piqued. Leon had told me we could make a lot of money together. But he had assured me it wouldn't involve prostitution. Now why in the world were we headed for a funeral home?

When Leon didn't offer any explanation and when my curiosity could no longer be contained, I leaned over and whispered, "Leon, what's up?"

His face saddened. "Oh, that's right; you probably hadn't heard. My mother just died. I've got to attend the wake."

Poor Leon! It would be bad enough just to face the death of his mother, but to undergo that terrible beating from Jimmy, too—it was too much. "I'm so sorry," I sympathized. "Did you and your mother have a good relationship?"

"I had the greatest mom in the world. If I came home late at night, she would be up waiting for me, usually with some kind of snack or something. She never nagged me; always tried to bring out the best in me. She bailed me out of jail once; took me to clinics; did everything a mother could do—even though I knew I was hurting her at times. I'm certainly going to miss her. Her death was such a shock."

I sat there wondering what it was like to have a good relationship with your mother. If my mom had died, I'd probably be glad!

"Here we are, folks," the cab driver announced. Leon

paid her, giving a generous tip. Then we headed inside the gorgeously appointed foyer. A black-suited man asked if he could be of help.

"I'm here to attend the wake of Amelia Prout," Leon told him.

The man, looking startled, asked, "Amelia Prout? I'm sorry, sir, but we don't have a wake scheduled for any Amelia Prout. Are you sure you have the right name?"

"Right name!" Leon exploded. "Of course it's the right name; it's my mother! Now don't get smart with me, mister, or I might just do you in!"

His face flushed, he was so angry. And I sure didn't blame him.

"Sir," I interjected, "you're not up to some practical joke, are you? We've come to see Leon's mother's body."

"Friends, the funeral business is serious business," the man said, shifting his weight uneasily from one foot to the other. "This is no place for practical jokes. I am Mr. Cook, and I know what's going on here. I'm very sorry, but we simply do not have anyone named Amelia Prout here. Are you sure you've got the right funeral home?"

"Of course I have the right funeral home," Leon snapped. "This is Cook's, isn't it?"

"Yes, this is Cook's. But I don't have Amelia Prout here."

"Then who do you have?" Leon asked.

Walking to his desk, the man looked through a register of some kind. "We're making arrangements right now for three people," he said solemnly, "Elisabeth Pratt, Sheryl Libby, and Neil Freberg. So help me, sir, that's it."

"Who are those people again?"

"Elisabeth Pratt, Sheryl Libby, and Neil Freberg."

Leon repeated the names and then asked, "And you're

absolutely positive you don't have my mother here?"

As gently as possible the man said, "Sir, I am Mr. Cook. I own this funeral home. I assure you I am not hiding your mother. Maybe she is at Clarke's Funeral Home. People do get the names mixed up occasionally."

Leon looked very apologetic as he said, "I'm sorry; maybe my brother did say Clarke's. We can go over there. Or I can call him. I'm sure it's just a mix-up. I'm sorry."

As we headed back outside, I thought, *Poor Leon! What a crazy mix-up! He must be suffering terribly!*

Leon didn't say anything as we walked along. When a cab came by, he hailed it. He gave the driver an address on Arts Street, saying, "It's Dr. Talbot's office."

When we were settled in the cab, I whispered, "Leon, I thought we were going to Clarke's. Aren't you kind of mixed up?"

When he leaned away from me and started laughing uproariously, I wasn't prepared for that kind of response. Was he going out of his mind?

He laughed so hard that he started holding his side. "Vicki, you're something else! You really fell for it, didn't you?"

"What do you mean, fell for it?" I demanded angrily. "You mean to tell me your mom didn't really die?"

Leon grabbed at his side again. "I have to quit laughing," he said, "or I'm going to die from the pain in this side."

I knew I had been had. "Okay, Leon, level with me. But what I feel like doing is punching you in those sore ribs!"

He finally straightened up long enough to take my hand and say, "Come on, Vicki, can't you take a little practical joke? Of course my mom didn't die. But I got the names of three dead people."

"Dead people? Why do you need something stupid like the names of dead people? You some kind of a ghoul?"

Leon smiled wryly and said, "Sure beats being a pimp!" That's all he would tell me.

But when we got out of the cab at the address, we stood outside the office and Leon said, "Now this is part of my plan for us to make a lot of money. If you do it right, I'll split with you fifty-fifty."

Now he really had my curiosity aroused.

"We're going to walk into that doctor's office," Leon said. "While we're waiting, I'm going to throw myself on the floor and have a fit. All you have to do is to start yelling for the doctor to come quickly. As soon as he runs out of his office toward me, you run into his office, grab his prescription pad, and slip it into your purse. That's all you have to do. I'll take care of the rest."

I could understand stealing a prescription pad. But what in the world did this have to do with dead people's names? Leon was already heading up the stairs, so I didn't have time to ask.

Inside the doctor's office I noticed two people waiting. Leon walked to the little window where the nurse sat. "May I see the doctor?" he asked. "I'm having some problems with epilepsy and need an examination."

She asked for his name and some other information and told us it would be a few minutes before the doctor could see him. So we both sat down and began leafing through some of the ancient magazines.

After about fifteen minutes Leon walked back to the nurse. "Ma'am," he said, "I'm not feeling at all well. I think maybe I'm going to have a seizure. Do you think it'll be much longer?"

"It certainly shouldn't be, sir," she answered. "I could get the doctor for you right now if you can't wait."

"Well, I guess I can hold out a little longer," Leon said as he limped back over and sat down next to me. Then he whispered, "Okay. You ready?"

Before I could respond, he threw himself on the floor and began thrashing his feet and legs around wildly. He kicked the coffee table, and magazines and ashtrays flew everywhere. The coffee table crashed into a lamp table, and the lamp crashed to the floor.

The nurse came flying out to us. As she did, I darted toward the office yelling, "Doctor! Doctor! Come quick! Come quick!"

Before I even got to the first door, it came flying open. "Doctor! Doctor!" I yelled. "My friend is having a terrible seizure in the waiting room!"

When the doctor headed toward Leon, I darted into his office. Sure enough, there was the prescription pad. I grabbed it and stuck it into my purse.

When I hurried back to the waiting room, Leon was still kicking on the floor. Saliva drooled from the corners of his mouth. He sure was some fantastic actor.

Suddenly Leon went very still. The doctor waited a few moments, gently picked him up and helped him to a chair, and asked, "Are you all right now?"

Leon blinked his eyes and looked around sheepishly. "Where am I? Where am I?" he kept asking.

"You're right here in my waiting room," the doctor said. "Are you sure you're all right?"

Leon jumped to his feet and screamed, "What kind of a quack are you? I told your nurse I needed help. And you let me have a seizure. You ought to be arrested!"

"Sir, calm down," the doctor said. "We're here to help you. But you have to let us know how bad you are."

"I told your nurse I was about to have a seizure," Leon shouted. "She sat there and didn't do one thing!"

"Doctor, the young man did tell me he felt like he was about to have a seizure," the nurse responded. "I offered to get you right then. He was the one who decided he could wait for you."

Leon grabbed my arm and headed for the office door. "Let's get out of here, Vicki. I had heard this was a good doctor, but he's nothing but a quack. I sure don't want any doctor like this touching me!"

He jerked the office door open, pushed me through, and yelled, "People like this ought to be arrested!"

He slammed the door behind us so hard that the building seemed to shake. We were almost down the steps when the door opened again and we heard the doctor yell, "Come back, mister. It isn't necessary for you to go away like that. I'll help you!"

Leon didn't even turn around. But as soon as we turned a corner out of sight of the doctor, he whispered to me, "Did you get his prescription pad?"

"I sure did!" I said proudly. "It's right here in my purse."

"Let me have it."

Enough was enough. I had to find out what was going on. "Okay, Leon, I played the game, and I played it well. Now tell me, what's going on here?"

"You haven't figured it out? I'm surprised. Well, I'm going to write a phony prescription for forty Dilaudids in the name of Elisabeth Pratt, that dead woman."

"Why Elisabeth Pratt?"

"Some of these druggists are real dummies; others are

smart. The smart ones will go to the phone book and check out Elisabeth Pratt. Maybe they'll even call her to see whether she's the right one. Well, our Elisabeth Pratt isn't about to answer any telephone!"

"Why not just make up a name?"

"Vicki, I tried that once. But the name I made up happened to be a real name, and the druggist called the guy on the phone. You'd better believe I was in hot water on that one. So once I got out of the drugstore I vowed I'd never again use a fictitious name. Now I use only the names of people who have died recently."

After we had walked a few blocks, Leon spotted a drugstore and quickly wrote out a prescription and handed it to me. It certainly looked authentic. I couldn't read a word of it.

"How did you learn to write like that?"

He laughed. "That's a trick I learned in prison. We had a lot of time there with nothing to do. So some of us decided to learn to write prescriptions. Prison is like going to school and learning a trade. Well, I learned to write prescriptions for Dilaudids—just like the doctors do. And would you believe the guy I learned from was a doctor? He got busted for writing false prescriptions and selling them. I mean, this guy was real smart."

I couldn't help but wonder if the doctor was so smart, what was he doing in prison? But I decided not to ask. It might make Leon mad. I didn't know yet how far I could push him.

Next, Leon pulled out his wallet and handed me a twenty-dollar bill. "I imagine the prescription will cost you around fifteen dollars," he said.

"I thought this was for forty Dilaudids," I countered.

"It is."

"What? You mean forty Dilaudids cost only fifteen dollars?"

"Yep."

"But, Leon, you charged me forty dollars each for them the other night."

He smiled. "That's right, baby. The price they cost and the price they bring on the street are far different. That's why I wanted you to work with me. We can spend fifteen dollars for forty Dilaudids and sell them for forty bucks each. That means we can make one thousand six hundred dollars on this deal—almost eight hundred dollars each, clear profit. Pretty good, huh?"

I simply couldn't believe it. That kind of a margin was incredible. Well, maybe not. We didn't have the Dilaudids yet.

The pharmacy was at the rear of the drugstore. When I handed the prescription to the druggist, my heart was beating like crazy. But I tried to act nonchalant.

He looked at the prescription, then went back to a shelf and started to search among the bottles. I recognized the Dilaudids as he pulled out a bottle and started counting them out. He handed the prescription bottle to me and said, "That'll be fifteen dollars and forty-five cents with the tax."

I handed him the twenty. In moments I had my change and the forty Dilaudids in my purse, and we walked out. I couldn't believe how absolutely simple the whole thing was. No questions, no phone calls, no nothing.

Leon and I caught a bus back to Bourbon Street and started peddling the Dilaudids. Later we went to his apartment and used some of them to get off ourselves.

Now that we were business partners, Leon suggested I might as well just live with him at his apartment. And since

I didn't have anywhere else to stay, it was an offer I couldn't refuse. At least I didn't have to go out and sell my body every night.

We kept hitting various drugstores with our phony prescriptions. Things had been going almost too well, and that made me nervous.

One day, with Leon standing close by, I handed a druggist a phony prescription. He started working on it, then turned to me and asked, "What is your name?"

I had just started to form the *V* for Vicki, but I caught myself. "My name is Elisabeth Pratt—with an *s*, not a *z*."

"Oh, yes, how dumb of me," the druggist said. "It's right here on the prescription." I smiled, but inwardly I knew something was wrong.

The druggist went to the back, and I couldn't see him. Then I spotted him at the end of another aisle. What was the matter with him? Didn't he know where the Dilaudids were?

Walking back to the counter where I was waiting, he said, "Ma'am, I'm sorry for the delay, but I will have to get these from the storeroom. I don't seem to have any of this drug up front."

When he walked toward the back, I glanced over and noticed Leon wipe his forehead. Then he moved next to me and whispered, "Let's get out of here now. This is a setup!"

As we darted for the front door, I said, "Are you sure? The guy said he didn't have any Dilaudids up front. And those drugs will bring us sixteen hundred bucks."

He didn't answer. He just kept pushing me toward the street. We hurried along for a couple of blocks and then crossed the street. As we did, we saw a blue car bearing down on us and we both jumped back. "Dumb, stupid driver!" I complained. "He ought to be arrested."

When we got safely across the street, Leon turned me in the direction of the drugstore and pointed. "Take a look, baby."

The blue car had pulled up in front of the drugstore and two guys jumped out.

"The dirty druggist called the cops!" Leon exclaimed. "We've got to get out of here!"

Fortunately for us a cab came along, and we hailed it. We drove right in front of that drugstore and saw the two detectives come rushing out of the front door and look up and down the street. I knew they were looking for us.

Yep, Leon was smart—and his smartness had kept us from getting caught. But that was almost too close. I just knew that one of these times we were going to get busted. Maybe the cops had put two and two together about prescriptions from Dr. Talbot. Now what were we going to do?

4

I sure felt good when that taxi got us back to Leon's apartment, safe and secure—at least for now. But I kept wondering how long it would be before we got caught. I knew the cops were looking for me because of that tavern robbery. Now they would be looking for me because of those false prescriptions.

I discovered it wasn't any fun being a fugitive from the law. No matter where you went, it seemed that every time you went around a corner, a cop might be standing there waiting for you.

And yet, getting caught might be a relief. At least I wouldn't be running anymore.

I tried to keep my mind off the possibility of getting caught by shooting up some of those Dilaudids we had. Leon and I always kept some of each prescription back so we could have our own drugs, and fortunately we had enough to last us for a time without having to write any more prescriptions.

Leon was a smart dude. He was thirty and had been on the street most of his life, he told me. The time he had served in prison made him smarter in the ways of crime. But I could sense he got pretty nervous around the cops because he knew prison was no picnic, and he worried about getting busted again.

Leon was hooked on Dilaudids, too. I had tried cocaine a couple of times, but it just didn't work for me. When I got my rush, it made me go way up—and that was hard for me to handle. I needed a downer rather than an upper. And so did Leon.

One night Leon noticed the large scar on my stomach and wanted to know how I got it. "Oh, I was in a fight with this girl," I told him, "and she pulled a knife and really cut me up."

"Wow!" he responded, "I don't think I've ever seen a scar that long. You must have really been cut up on the inside."

"Yeah, I sure was. That knife cut my guts in twelve different places. The doctors had a nightmare trying to get me back together again."

Then I started to laugh.

"What's so funny?"

"Leon, I was just giving you a taste of your own medicine. I really didn't get into a knife fight. I'm scared to death of knives. But when I was fifteen, I had some problems with my colon, and the doctors had to operate."

Leon started rubbing the scar, asking, "Is that so? You sure it was just your colon?"

"Well, that's what the doctor said. And it seems to be all right now—although I do have a little pain there once in a while."

When he kept rubbing, I said in disgust, "What's the matter with you? You a pervert or something?"

"Didn't I ever tell you I almost became a doctor?" he said. "In fact, I was ready to graduate from medical school, and I did a really dumb thing. I mean, it was stupid."

Leon, a doctor? I knew he was smart. Sure, he easily could have been a doctor.

"What happened?"

"Oh, a bunch of us students were in the dorm one night

goofing off because we were getting near the end of med school. We got some Dilaudids and started to mainline them. We all got high, and the faculty found out about it. Six of us were thrown out of school. And, baby, when that happens to you in the medical profession, you might as well hang it up. There's no way we could get back in.

"You know," he continued thoughtfully, "doctors have a funny thing about their profession. As soon as a doctor starts taking drugs, immediately he is isolated. So my medical career ended before it even got started."

Too bad. Leon would have made a good doctor. And I could have been a doctor's wife. We wouldn't have to keep running from the law, and we could be living in luxury. But could I live without my drugs?

As Leon continued rubbing my scar, it began to tingle. "It sure is ugly, isn't it?" I said.

"Yeah, it is ugly. I could have done a much better job on you. Your doctor must have been a real hack."

Then Leon started pushing in on the scar and on more spots on my stomach. "As I push in here," he said, "do you feel something in there?"

Yes, there was a slight discomfort.

"How long have you had this lump?" he asked.

I looked down. My stomach was always kind of bloated. But I sure wasn't aware of any lump.

"What lump?"

He pushed a little more. "It's inside there. Have you had it for quite a while?"

"For the life of me, I didn't know I had it at all. Maybe it's always been there. What do you think it is?"

He kept probing. "That lump really bothers me, Vicki."

"What do you mean, bothers you? It's my lump! But it's probably just some gas."

Looking very serious, Leon said, "Vicki, I don't want to scare you, but that lump could be cancer."

"Cancer? You're kidding me!"

"Calm down," he said, pushing me back down. "While I was studying medicine, cancer was one of the things I specialized in. I had big plans. I decided I was going to find the cure for cancer. Vicki, in my examination of many patients, I noticed a lump like that quite often. I really suspect it is cancerous."

I couldn't believe it. I had told Grandma I was going to die a junkie, but I wasn't! I would die of cancer!

It made me think of my Aunt Venice. She had died a slow, torturous death with cancer years ago. And once Mom thought she had cancer. She said it ran in the family.

"What am I going to do now?" I moaned in desperation.

"Well, I suppose you will have to have an operation. It could be very painful, so you are going to have to have a lot of pain killers."

I thought of the Dilaudids. They certainly took away the pain. Evidently Leon had the same thing in mind. "I guess you could stay on Dilaudids," he said, "so you can live without pain. I guess that's the only thing you can do."

At least now I had an excuse for my drug habit. I would have to have Dilaudids to take away the pain. So until I died I could at least stay high!

Then Leon shared with me a plan for us to get the Dilaudids I needed—and some extra for him, too.

The next morning we rented a car and drove to Baton Rouge, where we went to a hospital emergency room. I asked the receptionist, "Ma'am, could I see a doctor, please? I have cancer and need some medication."

She looked at me suspiciously. Then she looked at Leon. Did she suspect we were trying to get drugs for our habits?

Well, to me it really didn't make any difference. I had a reason for taking them now.

She motioned for us to sit down and in a few minutes called me in to see the doctor.

After I told him my problem, he examined me and asked what I needed. Without a moment's hesitation I said, "I have been taking Dilaudids for the pain."

When he asked, "Who is your doctor?" I had to think quickly.

"Oh," I said, "my husband and I are down here visiting my sister. We're from Maine. My doctor there is Dr. Brennan. You see, my sister had a baby, and we came down to stay with her. But she's really had a rough time, and we had to stay longer than we expected. I'm all out of Dilaudids, and obviously I can't get back to Maine to refill my prescription. I have really been in a lot of pain the last couple of days. I thought I could hold out, but it keeps getting worse. I've got to have something now."

"I'm sorry," he said, "but I can't prescribe that drug unless I take some X rays and run some other tests."

"Doctor, for crying out loud, you can see I'm in agony," I cried. "Why don't you just call Dr. Brennan? Honest, we can't afford to spend any more on X rays and tests. I am still trying to pay off the cost of my last operation and all the X rays and tests and medicine. I feel so guilty because my illness is taking every penny my poor husband makes. And with the cost of coming down here and then having to stay extra time, we're really strapped. Please, doctor, just give me the prescription. I'll be back home in a week. Dr. Brennan will continue to care for me, then."

I guess I sounded convincing because he went over to his desk and began to write on his prescription pad. As he handed the prescription to me, he said, "Here; I really don't have time to take on another patient, anyway. I sure hope everything works out okay for you."

I grabbed the prescription, thanked him, and Leon and I headed for a local drugstore.

"You keep your eyes out for the cops," I said, "because this makes me nervous."

He laughed. I interrupted with, "You think you're going to run forever and never get busted, don't you? Well, you'd better wise up, mister. One of these days your foolishness will trip you and we are going to get busted."

"Vicki, Vicki, just think about what we did. Just think about where we are going. Just think."

I was thinking. But I was thinking about the cops who had almost caught us at that drugstore in New Orleans. And it surprised me that Leon wasn't as smart as I was.

Taking my arm, Leon explained, "Vicki, that prescription you have is legitimate. The doctor's examination was legitimate. And so all we are going to do is to go into this drugstore and buy some legitimate Dilaudids with a legitimate prescription. This druggist isn't going to call any cops. Why should he? If he has any questions, he can call the doctor; and the doctor will verify the prescription. When the doctor does that, we are on our way! That's the beautiful part of your having cancer!"

The word *cancer* made me explode inside. Before I knew what I was doing, I smacked Leon across the face and blubbered, "Don't ever say that word to me again. Don't you know I'm dying? Don't you care? All you think about is getting these drugs."

I half expected Leon to hit me back, but he just stood there—smiling. At least he could show some sympathy for me. Maybe he really didn't care whether I lived or died.

"I'm sorry, Vicki," he finally said. "I'll never use that

word again. And I'll do everything I can to make these last days of yours as pleasant as possible. I will love you as you've never been loved before."

I dried my tears and made my way to the pharmacy. Leon was right. We had absolutely no hassle in getting the prescription filled. Another forty Dilaudids.

Back in New Orleans we sold some and kept the rest for our own use. But even the frequent highs didn't keep me from feeling my stomach. I just knew that lump was getting bigger by the day.

For a whole month Leon and I would drive to some small-town hospital, and I would give the same story. The crazy thing was that it worked every time!

But one evening I was terribly depressed. The cancer was getting bigger, and I knew my days were numbered.

Leon noticed me pushing on the lump and said, "Vicki, I wish you would stop that. It makes me nervous."

I couldn't believe the guy was so unfeeling. "Makes *you* nervous?" I repeated sarcastically. "What do you think it's doing to me? I'm the one who's dying, and you have the gall to sit there and say I'm making you nervous. Leon, I haven't got much longer in this life. Why don't you start showing me some of that love and sympathy that you promised?"

When he started laughing, I raised my hand to slap him. But he grabbed my arm, spun me around, and threw me to the floor, face down. I felt horrible pain in my stomach and screamed, "Leon! Leon! Don't hurt me! Please don't hurt me! That cancer is all through my body, and the pain is killing me. Please!"

He kept laughing, and I screamed, "How inhuman can you get? I'm dying!"

He had been sitting on my back, but he got off and rolled

me over. Looking me straight in the eye he said, "Vicki, do you know something?"

"Do I know what?"

"Vicki, you don't have cancer."

"What do you mean, I don't have cancer? You know I do. You felt that lump. You know it's getting bigger and bigger. You don't have to try to make things easier by lying to me."

He laughed again. I would have slapped him, but he had both my arms pinned to the floor as he sat on my stomach.

I gritted my teeth in pain. "Please get off my stomach. You're killing me."

"Okay, Vicki, but I am going to level with you. Here's the story."

"What do you mean, level with me?" I said, turning on my side and rubbing my stomach to ease the pain.

"This whole thing is getting out of hand," he said. "First, I am no doctor. Second, I have never been to medical school. I made the whole thing up."

"You did what?" I asked incredulously. I pushed myself to a sitting position on the floor and stared at him.

"I learned that cancer trick in jail," he said.

"You mean you've never been to medical school?"

"No. You see, the whole thing was all up here." He pointed to his head. "You were such an easy setup. When I started probing around on your scar, I simply used the power of suggestion. I suggested there was a lump there. Now, Vicki, we have many lumps in that area of our body. I set you up by giving you credentials of my supposed medical experience. You know, doctors say that maybe as much as ninety percent of sickness is in people's heads. So I led you to believe you had cancer. So help me, I'll bet you a million dollars that you don't have a single trace of cancer in your body. The whole thing is in your mind."

So I'd been had again. But I still had that lump in my stomach. It was there. I could feel it.

"Probably gas," Leon said.

Then I realized what he was doing. "I know you, Leon. You're saying all this just to help me to feel better. But I really do have cancer. Right?"

"Wrong. But there's only one way to find out. Tomorrow we'll take you down for a complete physical—a legitimate one."

I still didn't know what to believe. But the next day we did go to a doctor who examined me thoroughly. I went through a whole series of tests and X rays. And Leon was right. No cancer. I was both relieved and upset. Relieved because I didn't have cancer. Upset with Leon for leading me on like that and letting me endure such mental anguish.

"I think we've pretty well covered the area hospitals," Leon said that afternoon. "I think we'd better lay low on your story about being a cancer victim. Besides, maybe you won't sound so convincing now that you know the truth."

I was all for giving up that one. It had taken a lot out of me. And I knew a few of the doctors were suspicious. Maybe some of them had called the cops.

The following afternoon Leon motioned me close as he made a phone call. "Get right up next to my head," he told me. "I want you to listen to the response from the receiver, too."

I leaned up against his ear and heard the operator say, "Memorial Hospital."

"May I speak with the nurse in the emergency room, please?" Leon asked.

In a moment another woman's voice answered, "Hello."

"Is this the emergency room?"

"Yes."

"Which doctor is in charge of the emergency room today?"

"Dr. Webber."

"May I speak with him, please? This is Dr. Willis Reed calling. And what is Dr. Webber's first name, please?"

"It is Dr. Walter Webber."

"Thank you," Leon answered. "And, oh, yes. Do you know where Dr. Webber studied medicine?"

The nurse laughed. "Yes," she said. "Both of us are graduates of Baylor."

"You're kidding!" Leon said. "That's where I studied!"

There was a long pause. Then the nurse asked, "What did you say your name was again?"

"Reed. Willis Reed. When were you in school?"

The nurse giggled. "Oh, I just got out last year."

"My goodness, I've been out for ten years," Leon said. "It's been a long time since I talked with Dr. Webber."

"Just a moment; I'll get him for you."

Leon sure was a convincing liar.

In a few moments a man's voice said, "Dr. Webber here. May I help you?"

"Dr. Webber, this is your old friend Dr. Willis Reed."

There was a long pause before Dr. Webber replied, "Yes, Dr. Reed. What can I do for you?"

"Walter, for crying out loud, don't you remember me? This is Willis. Willis Reed."

How was poor, old Dr. Webber going to remember somebody who didn't exist?

"Walter, you and I were students together at Baylor," Leon went on. "Actually, you were a year ahead of me, but I always admired your ability. I used to live down the hall from you. In fact, I think we may have dated the same girl. I dropped her, but I was wondering if maybe you married her. She always seemed as though she cared the most about you."

"Well," Dr. Webber answered, "I did marry one of the girls from school. Her name is Becky."

"That's her!" Leon exclaimed. I don't know if she ever told you we had dated a few times. Man, she is a wonderful girl. You sure were lucky to get her!"

"Well, thank you, doctor."

"But I'm happily married, too," Leon went on. "I've got a wonderful wife—Camille. I met her while I was doing my internship."

Then Leon got to the point of his call. "Walter, I'm calling from my office in Dallas. I just got a call from a patient of mine, Vicki Hensley. It's kind of a sad story, but she's got cancer. It looks terminal."

"Too bad, Willis. Seems like I'm getting more and more cases like that myself. Sure hope someday they'll find a cure."

"Yes, I know what you mean on that one," Leon answered. "But I was wondering if you could do me a little favor. Vicki is down there in New Orleans visiting, and she had to stay a little longer than she had planned on. She tells me she's in terrible pain. I've had her on Dilaudids to ease it. They seem to work best for her."

I jerked my head back and looked at Leon admiringly. This guy was a real brain!

"I wonder if you'd mind if I sent her down to you," Leon said. "Maybe you could take a look at her and help her with a prescription. Would that be all right?"

There was a long pause. Would Dr. Webber fall for it?

Then he mumbled, "Yeah, I guess so. I really don't like giving out this kind of medicine unless I really know the patient."

"Well, I can sure appreciate that caution, Walter. But I'll tell you what. You do me this favor, and the next time you're in Dallas, be sure to look me up. I'll take you to lunch. How about that?"

Dr. Webber laughed. "Well, I guess I should do something to help a fellow alumnus."

"I really appreciate this favor," Leon said. "And I know Vicki will, too. She's a nice little gal, and I feel so bad about her problem. This cancer is a terrible thing. I know you understand."

"Oh, no problem, no problem," Dr. Webber responded. "And the next time I'm in Dallas, I'll give you a call."

"Thanks, Walter. And when I get down to New Orleans, I'll look you up, too."

Leon hung up the phone, his face mirroring his latest triumph.

"Are you sure you didn't study medicine?" I asked. "You even sound like a doctor."

Leon laughed. "Vicki, now don't get mad, but I've had to lie to you in order for us to get drugs. I really did study medicine at Baylor. But I got thrown out of the medical profession for taking drugs. Besides, I never could learn how to play golf."

I stared in disbelief. It was getting more and more difficult to figure this guy out. Was he lying, or was he telling the truth? And which part was lies, which part the truth?

"Leon, are you putting me on again? Are you really Dr. Willis Reed going by an alias? Or are you Dr. Leon Prout?"

"Vicki, Vicki, you are so gullible," Leon laughed. "I wasn't a doctor. I don't have enough patience to be one."

I was going to make a pun on doctors having to have patients. But instead I punched his arm and said, "Leon, I don't know what I am going to do with you. You are the biggest liar, the biggest con artist I have ever met!"

"Thank you, madame," he said, grinning. Then he told me to get ready to go on down to the hospital. "I'm anxious for you to meet my good friend and medical-school colleague, Dr. Walter Webber."

As we headed for the hospital, I wondered if Dr. Webber was going to go along with the story. He had sounded rather cagey to me. Suppose he had called Dallas to see if there really was a Dr. Willis Reed. And if he had found out there was no such doctor, undoubtedly he would have called the cops. This was still a highly dangerous caper.

I suppose that's why I was nervous when, in the hospital emergency room, I noticed a guy dressed in a suit leaning up against the wall. Was he a detective?

"Leon," I whispered as I poked him with my elbow. "Don't look right this minute. But notice that guy over to the left there. The one in a suit, standing up against the wall. Is that a cop?"

Leon went on reading a magazine, but he stole a glance in that direction. "Yeah," he finally answered. "That's a detective if I ever saw one."

I grabbed Leon's arm and urged, "Let's get out of here now! This is a setup!"

He patted my arm and said, "Just stay cool, Vicki. You'll often see cops in hospital emergency rooms. He probably brought an accident victim in or somebody who may have been hurt when he was arrested. There are always cops around here. Don't worry."

But when I glanced back over, the detective was staring right at us. My heart started to beat like crazy.

"Leon, I don't care what you say, this is a setup. We'd better get out of here while we can."

"Not to worry, Vicki. That cop is here for something else."

"I'm nervous, Leon, real nervous. This may be the end; that guy may be waiting to bust us."

"You go see my friend Dr. Webber," he said. "I'll take care of the cop."

"Sure, sure, you'll take care of the cop. He's waiting to take care of me! They're waiting for Vicki Hensley, not Leon Prout!"

"Vicki, I've never steered you wrong. So listen to me. I know what I'm doing. This is too good an angle to let go now."

Maintaining a firm grip on my arm, Leon pushed me toward the nurse at the desk. When she looked up, I said, "May I see Dr. Walter Webber, please? He's expecting me."

The nurse nodded, got up, and headed for a back room. But I noticed that when she did, that detective followed her! I just knew that at any minute both of them were going to come back—and I was going to get busted!

5

I was so nervous waiting for that nurse to get back that I started to pace. Why did the detective go back there with her? When I passed Leon, I whispered, "So help me, if that detective grabs me, I'll kick him right where it hurts and run for it!"

"Just stay cool, Vicki," Leon cautioned. "And quit worrying. Nothing is going to happen."

"Sure, Leon, sure," I replied, "nothing's going to happen. It's not going to happen to you. But I have to go back there into that doctor's office while you just sit here. You can get away easy; I'm a sitting duck!"

By this time I was standing by the emergency-room door—I guess I felt safer in a spot where I could run for it if I had to. Leon casually walked over by me and pulled back his shirt just a little. Tucked inside his belt was my .357 magnum. Smart guy! Why hadn't I thought of that? I should have carried it in the first place.

"You've got my word, Vicki," Leon said, "if that detective tries anything, I'll drop him in his tracks!"

Before he knew what was happening, I had grabbed the gun from him. "Careful," he cautioned. "It's loaded!"

He didn't have to tell me that. He'd have been a fool to have carried it if it wasn't loaded. Quickly I stuck it in my purse. I didn't want anybody else seeing it.

Well, Leon grabbed my purse to try to get the gun back. That started a big tug of war with Leon saying in a low voice, "Vicki, you don't understand! I'm doing this for your own good. If that is a cop in there and they bust you, the first thing they'll do is search your purse. They'll be looking for drugs, for your works, stuff like that they can charge you with. And, baby, when they find that .357 magnum in there, it's all over for you. Please don't go in there with that gun!"

I still had a firm grip on my purse as I answered, "If I've got to go into that doctor's office and that detective pulls a smart one, there's going to be a shoot-out. No way am I going to jail!"

When I emphasized that last point with my hands, I slightly relaxed my grip on the purse, and Leon flipped it out of my hands and behind his back. Just as I lunged for it, a voice behind me said, "Okay, miss, Dr. Webber is ready to see you."

Leon stood there smugly. The nurse was waiting. But I wasn't about to go back there without that gun.

"Nurse, do you know this man standing here?" I asked as I pointed at Leon.

"No, ma'am."

"Well," I continued, "I don't know him, either. Would you please ask him to give me back my purse or else call the cops?"

When the nurse looked at Leon, he sheepishly said to me, "But, Vicki, you know who I am."

"Nurse," I said, "I have no idea who this man is. But he just snatched my purse."

"Mister," the nurse said, "I don't know what is going on here, but I think you'd better give that purse back to the lady."

He knew he was outfoxed, so he handed the purse to me. But as he did, he said in a low voice, so that only I could hear, "You're stupid, Vicki. You'll be sorry!"

I wrinkled up my nose at him, and, hugging the purse tightly, I followed the nurse down the hall. Maybe I was stupid, like Leon said. But I wasn't about to be a fool!

As I walked, I kept snatching glances around to see if I could spot that detective. But I couldn't see him anywhere. Leon was probably right; the detective was on another case. It was just a coincidence that he went down the hall when the nurse did.

Finally the nurse opened a door and motioned me inside an office. The doctor stood as I entered. Sticking out his hand, he said, "I'm Walter Webber. I understand you're a patient of a friend of mine. Is that right?"

"Yes, sir," I said, "and he just called me and told me that he thought you might be able to help me out."

"Well, we'll see what we can do," he replied. "Let me see. What was your doctor's name, again? I have such a terrible memory for remembering names, and I guess I hadn't heard from him since medical school. I've been having trouble placing him."

Oh, no! I was so busy thinking of how clever Leon's little ruse was that I had forgotten to memorize the name he had used. How could I possibly be so stupid!

I started to mumble something, and then I blurted out, "Oh, I'm feeling a little dizzy. The room is starting to go on its side!"

I staggered a little and then slumped to the floor. I closed my eyes, hoping I remembered enough what a faint was like so that I could fake it.

I could sense Dr. Webber kneeling beside me. With his thumb he opened one eyelid. I tried not to look at him and kept forcing my eyeball up to the top of my head. Then he did the same thing to my other eye. I forced that eyeball up.

But it came down, and I looked right at him. So I started blinking and asking blankly, "Where am I? Where am I?"

He stood straight up and looked down at me. "Young lady, you're in my office. Are you all right?"

I opened my eyes wide and looked around as if I were seeing everything here for the first time. Then I said, "Oh, yes, you're Dr. Webber. Goodness me, the last thing I remember is walking in here. What happened? Why am I on the floor?"

He didn't respond. As I rolled over to get to my feet, I expected him to be gentleman enough to at least extend a hand to help me up. But he just stood there. I finally struggled to a nearby chair.

"Now what's the matter, young lady?"

I needed to tell him that my doctor in Dallas said I had cancer and had been giving me Dilaudids for the pain. But what was the name Leon used? Maybe Dr. Webber really didn't remember. Maybe he wouldn't know the difference if I made up a name.

"Didn't Dr. Burton tell you?" I asked.

"Dr. Burton? That doesn't sound like the name of the man who called me." He walked to his desk, pushed some papers aside, and pulled out a handwritten note. "Oh, here it is. I received a call from Dr. Willis Reed. I don't know any Dr. Burton."

Thinking fast, I replied, "Oh, sure, it was Dr. Reed who called. Dr. Burton is his associate. I usually see Dr. Burton, but since Dr. Reed was the one who knew you, he offered to call. I do see Dr. Reed part of the time, so he knows my case well. And Dr. Reed is really a wonderful man."

I sensed I wasn't getting along too well. Was Dr. Webber

onto our scheme? Well, at least that detective wasn't around.

"Come with me into the next room," Dr. Webber said. "I'll have to give you a brief examination."

"Examination?" I responded. "I don't see why you need to do that. All I'm asking for is some medicine for my pain. I'll be going back to Dallas, and—"

"Young lady," Dr. Webber interrupted, "I know all that. But surely you know that I can't give you a prescription for something like Dilaudids without giving you an examination. You must be smarter than that."

"Oh, I see. You're not just in the business of writing out prescriptions, are you?"

"Now, young lady, if you're inferring that I'm trying to make a little extra money off you, you're barking up the wrong tree. What I'm trying to tell you is that these are days when junkies are ripping off doctors right and left. One of my colleagues just got busted. He's going to have to do time because he was very foolish in writing prescriptions for dangerous drugs. So no way am I going to do some foolish thing and write prescriptions that could ruin me professionally."

This doctor was smart—maybe too smart.

In the next room he motioned me onto the examination table. I did as he said, but I held my purse close. In fact, I kept two fingers on the zipper—just in case!

"I'll have to ask you to take off your blouse," Dr. Webber said. "And, here; let me take that purse. I'll lay it down over here where you can keep an eye on it."

He took the purse to move it, but I hung on tightly.

"My goodness, you must have gold or diamonds in there, the way you're hanging onto it," he said. "But there just isn't room for it and you on this little examination table. I promise I'm not going to steal anything from it."

He sounded so convincing. With a quick jerk he pulled the purse out of my hands and set it on a table. Then he asked me again to slip off my blouse.

When I did, he took hold of my arm and looked at my armpit. "What's this?" he asked.

He had his finger right on my track. And he sure didn't need me to explain what it was he was seeing. Did he suspect what I was up to?

"Doctor, I'll level with you," I said. "I used to be a drug addict, but I'm not anymore. When I found out I had cancer, I decided to go straight. My parents have been so upset about the cancer that I didn't want to lay anything else on them. That's an old track."

Rubbing the surface of it he said, "Looks fresh to me."

He didn't say anything else about it but with his stethoscope began to check my heart. I kept glancing at my purse.

"Okay, you can put your blouse back on," he finally said. "I can't really find anything wrong with you. I just hope this doctor of yours isn't a quack. But I'll write you out a prescription for twenty Dilaudids."

"Dilaudids?" I asked. "What are they for? Are they bitter?"

"Young lady," he said, and there was a ring of disgust in his voice, "I don't know whether you're for real or not. But I think there's a couple of things we ought to get straight. First, you didn't faint when you came into my office. That was a phony faint if ever I saw one. Second, those are fresh tracks on your arm. Third, I don't mess with junkies. If you say you're sick, I'll take your word for it. If you say you have cancer, I'll take your word for that. I'm just trying to stay out of trouble—with the cops and with the junkies. I'm going to give you this prescription, and I want you to get out of here. And I don't ever want you to come back again. Do you understand?"

I nodded. I was really anxious to get out now—before he called the cops on me.

"I'll be back in a minute," he said. "You wait here."

He walked back into his office, leaving the door open so I could see him. Good! He was writing on his prescription pad! I had made it! No cops!

He walked back in and handed me the prescription. I quickly unzipped my purse and stuck the prescription inside.

As I did, he stepped beside me and said, "Another thing, young lady; don't ever come into a hospital emergency room carrying a gun. You see, when I grabbed your purse, I immediately felt the gun. That's another reason I don't mess with junkies. Sometimes they pull guns on you. Sometimes they pull knives. There's no telling what they are likely to do, and I just want to stay out of the whole thing. I have a wife and three kids who are depending on me, and I want to keep it that way. I'm not going to put my life and my reputation on the line for some junkie."

What could I say? I had what I wanted, so I turned to leave.

"What kind of a gun do you carry?" Dr. Webber asked.

Startled, I turned around. "A .357 magnum. It's a real good gun."

"You're kidding," he said in surprise. "A .357 magnum? I've always wanted one, but I haven't had time to go through all the hassle you have to go through to get one. Say, can I work a deal with you?"

"You mean you want my gun?"

He nodded. I was shocked. Up to this point the guy had seemed so honest, so totally above board. Now he was offering to make a dishonest deal. Maybe I could use this to my immediate advantage—and even a little blackmail down the road!

"How bad do you want it?"

"Name your price."

"Give me two more prescriptions for forty Dilaudids each, and the gun is yours."

"Two more prescriptions? That's an awfully big price for a gun."

"Doctor, you aren't looking at it right," I replied. "Actually you are getting the gun free. After all, I've got to go out and buy those Dilaudids. All you have to do is give me two pieces of paper with your writing on them. It sounds to me like that's a fantastic deal for you."

"It's not quite that simple," he replied. "After all, my reputation is at stake every time I write a prescription. I could lose my license over something like this. But I think I could cover on this one because of your doctor in Dallas— Dr. Reed. I guess I'd be okay."

With that he walked back to his desk, quickly wrote out two more prescriptions, and came back and handed them to me. I unzipped my purse, stuffed the prescriptions inside, and handed him the gun. As he held it, he seemed to fondle it lovingly. "Wow! This is a fantastic one!" he told me.

"Careful!" I cautioned. "It's loaded."

He stood there checking every part of the gun, so I turned to leave. I was just about to put my hand on the doorknob when he said, "Oh, I forgot to tell you. Those prescriptions can be filled only at a certain drugstore. I'd better write the address down for you."

He went back to his desk and started writing something. He tried to do something else unobtrusively, but I noticed him push a button on a little machine on his desk. Was he calling the nurse for something?

I was really getting nervous now, but he kept writing. I couldn't leave without that address or these three prescriptions would do me absolutely no good. And I would have lost my gun, besides.

Just then the office door opened. I turned toward it, half expecting to see the nurse. But, no! It was that detective! I tried to run into the doctor's office, hoping to make it out the other door. But before I could move a step, that detective grabbed me, threw me against the wall, spun me around, and had handcuffs on me. It happened so fast I couldn't believe it.

"Hey! What in the world is going on here?" I screamed. "I'm dying with cancer. Do you treat all your patients like this? You get those handcuffs off me this minute. I'll have my lawyer sue you and the police department and this hospital. And I'll sue this doctor. You let me go, right now!"

"I'm Detective Clarement, vice squad, New Orleans Police Department," he said calmly. "Before you say anything, let me read you your rights."

He pulled out a little card and read it. I knew I didn't have to say anything unless I had my lawyer present.

"Okay, okay!" I screamed. "I want my lawyer right now!"

"You'll have to come down to the police station first," he replied. "First we have to book you. Then you can call your lawyer."

"You don't have a thing on me!" I yelled.

The detective picked up my purse, which had fallen to the floor in the scuffle. "She's got three prescriptions in there," Dr. Webber told him.

That dirty doctor! But wait! I had something on him! That was my gun on his desk; he had purchased it illegally.

So I blurted out, "Listen, detective, you may bust me; but you'd better bust this doctor, too. Do you know what he just did?"

"No. What did this doctor do—give you a dirty examination?" the detective asked with a laugh.

"Don't get smart!" I shouted. "You see that gun on his desk? That dirty, filthy doctor got that from me for two phony prescriptions. He's as crooked as I am. Why don't you bust him, too? Or doesn't the law touch the rich and powerful?"

Dr. Webber picked up my gun and fondled it again. "Young lady," he said, "is this the gun you're talking about? You mean you owned this .357 magnum and sold it to me for two prescriptions? Is that what you're saying?"

I couldn't quite figure out his angle, but I knew I had him now. "Yes, that's what I'm saying. And you know it's the truth, don't you, Dr. Webber?"

The doctor smiled. "Detective Clarement, I must confess my wrongdoing to you and throw myself on your mercy. What this young lady has said is the truth. I admit to you that I gave her two prescriptions for forty Dilaudids each for this gun."

What a stupid doctor! Why wasn't he trying to lie his way out? Well, that was his problem, not mine.

"Okay, Clarement, you heard the man confess," I said. "Now slap some cuffs on him, too!"

"Dr. Webber," the detective said, "I need some handcuffs. I seem to have brought only one pair with me, and they are in use at the moment. Could you get a set for me somewhere so I can slap them on you?"

Dr. Webber put his right hand into his back pocket and drew it out with a pair of handcuffs in it. "Will these do?" he asked.

"What is going on here?" I demanded, startled by this unexpected turn of events. "What are you doing carrying handcuffs?"

Dr. Webber merely smiled. Then he stuck his other hand out toward me. In it was a shiny, metal badge.

"What are you doing with a badge?" I yelled.

"Allow me to introduce myself," he replied. "I am Detective Stracker, vice squad, New Orleans Police Department. Detective Clarement is my partner."

"You're a detective?" I asked in surprise—and horror. And it began to dawn on me that I had walked right into a setup! They had me.

"Yes, I'm a detective; I'm not a doctor. And when you and your friend first walked into the emergency room, we had hidden electronic screening devices—metal detectors, if you please. You set the thing off. That alerted us.

"The second thing is that you junkies really ought to wise up. Don't you know that the fake-doctor call trick that you pulled has been pulled here by five other junkies this week? It's gotten so bad at this hospital that we asked if we could set up a separate unit here to bust you junkies. That's how I became Dr. Webber."

"Okay, you're smart. But how did you know that telephone call wasn't for real?"

"Oh, yes, the telephone call. After that turkey called, posing as a classmate, we immediately called Dallas. There was no Dr. Willis Reed registered there. When you came in, you couldn't remember the name. And then that phony faint. I mean, it was so evident something was up.

"And I had to get your gun away from you because I didn't want anyone to get hurt. So I bought it from you. I figured I could do that because you junkies are so greedy."

It became evident that that was all he was going to tell

me about their operation because the two of them pushed
me out of the room and down the hall.

That's when I thought about Leon. Had they already
busted him?

As we went through the waiting room, I looked around,
but I couldn't see him anywhere. I still didn't know
whether he had escaped or they had already taken him in.

Out in the parking lot the two pushed me into the backseat of a police car and took off toward the station. About a
block down the road a cab passed us going the other way. I
just happened to glance at it. Was it Leon? I couldn't be
positive, but it sure looked like Leon in the backseat. I almost shouted for joy that at least he had gotten away. But I
bit my tongue. Maybe it wasn't Leon. But if he did get
away, would he show up at the jail and bail me out? Or
would he dare? I wasn't all that sure how much he really
cared about me.

When I got out of the car, still handcuffed, down at the
station, I felt so horrible. People kept staring at me. Some
even pointed. I wanted to kick them for their rudeness.

Inside, a sergeant asked for my name and address and
whether I had ever been arrested before. When I told him
no, he didn't look convinced.

Then they fingerprinted me—all four fingers on my right
hand. They put the prints on a statement and made me
sign it.

While this was going on, the two detectives who had arrested me filled out their report. The one who had posed as
the doctor stood around there in his white coat, white
pants, and white shoes. I'm sure people wondered what a
doctor was doing there. Well, I knew. He was a good-for-
nothing detective who had trapped me!

Next they took me to a little room and made a mug shot

of me. Now I really felt like a criminal. The whole process was so dehumanizing!

Then they took my fingerprints and started checking to see if I had ever been arrested before. While they were doing that, I was waiting on a hard, wooden bench, wondering if anyone cared what happened to me. Then a woman officer came and ordered, "Follow me."

Obediently I got up and followed her down a hall, around several corners—and then I saw them—the barred cells. This was where I was going to be—like an animal in a zoo!

We walked by several cells. When she finally opened a door, it creaked—just like in the movies. "You'll be in here for a little while," she said without feeling.

When I just stood there, I felt her hand against my back pushing me into the cell. Before I knew it, I was inside, and the cell door slammed behind me. The sound ricochetted all over the place. The officer turned the key in the lock and walked off without another word.

I stumbled over to the door and shook it in anger and frustration. That got me nowhere, so I turned to look over my new "home." The only thing in it was a hard, backless bench—for sitting and for sleeping, I guess.

Then a horrible loneliness and hopelessness engulfed me, and my tears flowed freely. How in the world had I ever gotten myself into a mess like this? Was this where all junkies ended up—in a dirty, dingy, rotten cell?

And what was going to happen to me, now? I sure didn't know. But I was scared to death!

6

After the matron brought me some bland food, which I really didn't feel much like eating, I made myself as comfortable as I could on that bare bench. I don't think there is any way a person could sleep on that thing, so I could hardly say I slept that night. I guess I had too much on my mind to be able to sleep even on the most comfortable mattress.

Next morning I was up before the sun. Where I was and what was likely to happen to me was beginning to hit me full force. The tears came again—tears of regret, remorse, anger, frustration. How many years would I have to spend in prison? I sure hoped they wouldn't throw the book at me.

The first rays of daylight made me aware of the sick green color the walls had been painted. Then as I glanced around, I noticed names and statements written or scratched into the walls—almost like a gas-station rest room.

Beside one name was scrawled, "I'll kill him when I get out." Whom did she mean? A detective? Her pimp? Maybe her husband? I wondered what human dramas had been enacted inside the disgusting green walls of this dirty cell. Should I scratch my name there, too?

I had a small file on my fingernail clippers—they hadn't taken them away from me—so I scratched my name into the paint. Then, I don't know why, but I also scratched,

"Out of the darkness of the night I found myself."

Crazy! Why would I write something like that? What did it mean? Well, one thing was certain; it was the darkness of the night for me. I sure was worried about the penitentiary. If I went there, I'd probably just get deeper into crime.

Later that morning when the matron came, she said, "Vicki Hensley, you are to be taken before the judge to be arraigned. They will tell you what the charges are against you. I sure hope it isn't too bad for you."

She put handcuffs on me and started to lead me down the hall. "Did you really mean what you said?" I asked.

"Listen, honey, I used to work in the Lousiana State Prison for Women," she told me. "I mean, you go up there innocent, and you come out guilty. You might not know much now, but by the time you've been through that prison, you'll know everything. And you'll be right back on the streets putting it all into practice!"

Somehow I sensed she was telling the truth.

"So, Vicki, this is the place to stop. I mean, right now. When you go before that judge, just hope he'll slap your wrists and let you go. But, honey, if it's a tough charge, may the Lord have mercy on you!"

My heart skipped a beat. Would the judge send me to the penitentiary and place me with all the lesbians, murderers, and perverted women? I couldn't live through that. I promised myself that if I got out of this one, I would go straight. I'd go right back home to my grandma and be a good girl. Then I thought how foolish I was for even entertaining any hope like that. They had too much on me. No way was I going to get out of this one easily.

The matron led me to the courtroom and sat beside me as we watched the parade of people going before the judge for all kinds of crimes. Most of the people were there for stealing. I heard only two drug charges. In fact, one of the girls who was busted for drugs was an acquaintance. As she walked by me, she said, "Vicki, what are you doing here?"

I started to blurt out all I had done, but I bit my tongue. I could see no sense in admitting my guilt.

Another matron sort of pushed this girl by me. But as she did, I said, "Hope you make out all right."

The matron who was with me smiled. I guess she realized I was using her words to me. But I meant it. I didn't know if she did.

Before long they called my name, and I stood before the judge. He heard the charges: buying drugs for the purpose of reselling them, possessing false prescriptions, carrying a concealed weapon without a permit, possession of a hypodermic needle. Hypodermic needle? Oh, no! I'd forgotten about the set of works I had in my purse. I wondered what else they had found. While I was wondering that, I heard the final charge: resisting arrest.

They really had me. I tried to look repentant, but the judge was unimpressed. No show of mercy at all. He set my bail at ten thousand dollars.

No way could Leon come up with that kind of money. And Grandma certainly couldn't. That meant I would be kept in detention until my trial date. Not a very pleasant prospect.

The matron led me back through the winding halls to that same dirty cell. She didn't say anything; I guess she realized what I realized: my condition was pretty hopeless. Before long I was certain to be on my way to the Louisiana State Prison!

When we got to my cell, she took off my handcuffs, motioned me inside, and slammed the door. Once again that hollow sound ricochetted down the hallways. Wasn't it possible just to close the door? Did they always have to slam it?

I walked over and stared at the wall and what I had written on it. Yes, even more now it was the darkness of night. But would I ever find myself?

That afternoon I was visited by someone from legal aid. He said the court had appointed him to be my lawyer. But he was so young that I didn't have confidence he would be able to do anything to help me.

He asked me a bunch of questions about my past life. I told him the truth when I felt like it and lied when I felt like it. I told him that I was at that hospital because I had cancer, that I was innocent, that all the charges against me had been trumped up to make the police look good.

"Okay, Vicki," he said, "then do you want to plead guilty or not guilty? Do you want to tell the judge you have cancer and have him order an investigation? What do you want to do?"

"Well," I said, "there's one thing for sure; I don't want to go to prison."

"Well, I don't want you to go there, either," he said. "But the first step is for you to decide how you want to plead."

"I don't know," I told him. "As far as I'm concerned, I'm not guilty."

"But, Vicki," he protested, "look at the evidence they've got. You sold a gun to that detective for two phony prescriptions—and admitted that you did it in the presence of another detective. They found those works in your purse. Any one of those charges could send you away for a long, long time. But with the combination of all those charges, I would recommend plea bargaining. I'll go to the district attorney's office and see if I can get some of the charges reduced or dismissed if you admit to just one. Maybe then we can get you off with a light prison sentence."

"Light?" I asked. "How long is a light sentence?"

"That all depends. If the judge is in a good mood that day, it could be six months. If his mood is bad, it could be fifty years. If the assistant district attorney wants to make an example out of you, it could be more. If he's busy and wants to get this over with, the judge could even dismiss the charges and put you on probation. You'd be out free."

Was this justice? Why should my sentence be determined by the mood of some judge or the case load of some assistant district attorney? Why wasn't there some way I would know exactly how long I was going to get, so I would know whether to fight or not?

I pondered the possibilities and asked, "What should I do?"

"Well, I really think you ought to let me try some plea bargaining," he said. "Let me see what they'll settle for; then I'll get back to you. Okay?"

I agreed. It sounded like the best way out of an impossible situation. Besides, I hadn't agreed to do what they proposed.

Later that afternoon two other men visited me—big guys. Right behind them was the matron. I just sat there staring at them through the bars.

"I'm Detective Leach," one of the men said. "Are you Vicki Hensley?"

I studied him. He sure looked like a mean one—I guess because he was so big and muscular. But why did a detective want to talk to me?

"No, I'm not Vicki Hensley. I'm Jane Fonda."

"Well, you're a spirited little thing, aren't you?" the detective asked patronizingly.

The matron interrupted sarcastically, "This is Vicki Hensley."

"Detective Forminio and I would like to talk to you. Is that okay?"

Had my legal aid already made a deal? That didn't make sense. He would be talking to the district attorney's office. These guys were detectives. I didn't know whether or not I could trust them. But I said, "Okay, so I'm not Jane Fonda. What do you turkeys want?"

Detective Forminio asked the matron to unlock the door. "I think this kid needs a little lesson," he told her.

When I heard that, I knew what to expect. They had come down here to beat a confession out of me. They'd slam me around the cell until I was willing to confess to almost anything. Then I'd have no chance at all for plea bargaining, and I'd be sent away for many, many years.

So as the matron unlocked the door and it swung open, I jumped atop the bench. If these brutes were going to lunge at me, at least I'd be higher than they were. And if they laid a hand on me, I'd be in a position to scratch their eyes out.

The two turkeys walked in and stood about three feet from me. The matron slammed the door and locked it and marched down the hall. I knew I was about to get it.

"Come back here!" I yelled at the matron. "If these guys touch me, I want a witness. No way are they going to beat a confession out of me!"

The matron didn't even turn around as she unlocked an outer door, stepped through it, and disappeared down the hall. I was on my own.

"Want to talk?" Detective Leach asked.

My lips tightened. I wasn't going to say one word.

"Vicki, we're going to level with you," Detective Forminio said. "With the charges against you, you're up for fifty years. Did you hear what I said? That's fifty years. That's because we're going to throw the book at you. We've got the evidence on the weapons charge, on the false prescription charge, and on the possession charge. The judge has just been waiting for somebody like you to make an example of to the rest of the junkies in New Orleans. So when you come before that judge, he is going to put you away for good. Do you realize that with a fifty-year sentence, you'll be over seventy years old when you get out—if you live that long!"

I couldn't believe what I was hearing. Fifty years! Were they telling me the truth? Well, they sure made it sound convincing!

Suddenly it occurred to me that maybe by this time they had linked me with that tavern robbery. Maybe that's what they were here for. Maybe they would try to get me to confess. I had to know whether they knew.

"That seems like a lot of years for some minor, little charges," I said. "Why, I'll bet if I went out and robbed a tavern or a convenience store, I wouldn't get that many years. How come?"

The two detectives looked at each other, and Detective Leach said, "Should we tell her?"

"Yeah, I guess we might as well lay it all on the line," Detective Forminio answered.

What did he mean by that?

"Listen, you two goons," I said, "I am sick and tired of your cat-and-mouse games. Tell me what you want and get out of here. And so help me, if you lay a hand on me, I'll scream police brutality to the judge and to my lawyer and to anybody who'll listen."

"Vicki, do you know a girl named Cecelia Laird?"

"Cecelia Laird? Never heard of her. Did you bust her for something?"

"Well, isn't that strange," Detective Forminio said sarcastically. "Cecelia claims to know a Vicki Hensley very well. In fact, she said that both of you used to work somewhere together. Let's see. Did she say a drugstore? Or a variety store? Maybe it was at McDonald's or Burger King? Oh, yes. I remember now. It was at Gross's Tavern. Isn't that right?"

I sure wasn't going to admit to any robbery! "Hey, if you came here because you think I know Cecelia Laird, you've got another thing coming. I've never worked in a tavern. I don't know the difference between a beer and a martini. It's probably somebody else with the same name. This is a big city, you know."

Detective Leach yelled, "Matron, would you come open the door, please?"

I breathed easier. All this had been short and sweet. They didn't get any confession out of me, and they hadn't pushed me around. I thought I had outfoxed them with that mistaken-identity bit.

I could hear the matron coming, and she was obviously in no hurry. I sat back down on the bench, waiting for my visitors to leave. She finally unlocked the door. But just as it opened, the two detectives grabbed me—one on each arm—and lifted me up. I started kicking and squirming.

"Come on, Vicki," Detective Leach said soothingly, "we just want to take you down the hall to our office to ask you a couple more questions. Don't make it tough."

He'd think tough ! I hauled off and kicked him in the leg just as hard as I could. The next thing I knew they had spun me around and slammed me against the side of the cell. I felt my arm bend back; Leach was squeezing my little finger, and the pain was about to kill me.

When I screamed, he yelled, "Listen, you little twerp. Now I'm going to bust you for attacking a cop! So you cool it, kid, or it'll be tough on you. You can scream to the judge all you want; he's heard that before. So one more silly thing like that, and I'll slap you silly!"

He had my face pushed up against the cement wall. I could feel the rough edges digging into my skin. I knew I was no match for these two, so I let my body go limp. They both caught my arms to keep me from sprawling on the floor. Then they half led, half carried me down the hall into a small office and plopped me into a chair. I knew where I was now—the interrogation room.

"Okay, Vicki, let's go through this once more," Detective Leach said. "Did you or did you not rob Gross's Tavern?"

I didn't answer. If I admitted it, they would attach that to all the other charges against me. I'd better deny it again.

"Okay, you guys," I said, "I'll level with you. No way did I rob any bar, regardless of how gross a bar it was." I paused. They didn't even smile. "The only bar I ever robbed was a Hershey Bar I shoplifted at a grocery store." I giggled, but they still didn't even smile.

"I guess you don't realize how serious this all is," Detective Forminio said. "We'll have to show you the evidence."

Evidence? What kind of evidence? They sure didn't have the money I took. I had spent all that long ago.

Detective Forminio was gone for a few minutes; Detective Leach didn't say a word during that time, so it seemed like an eternity because I was worried.

A few minutes later Forminio returned with a girl. Oh, no. It was Cecelia! Now they did have evidence!

"Cecelia Laird, do you recognize this girl here?" Detective Forminio asked her.

When I looked straight at Cecelia, she tried to avoid my eyes. Then she said what I had been dreading: "Yes, this is Vicki Hensley. This is the girl who robbed Gross's Tavern."

I jumped up and screamed, "You're a dirty, filthy liar! You're the one who robbed that tavern! I didn't do it!"

"Want to take a lie detector test?" Detective Forminio asked.

He had me. "Cecelia has already taken one," he went on. "She came out completely clean. Do you want to try, now?"

"There is no way, absolutely no way, I am going to admit to robbing any bar!" I screamed. "Absolutely no way!"

"Well, you can scream your innocence all you want, young lady," Detective Leach said, "but Cecelia Laird has agreed to testify against you in court. Armed robbery of a tavern should add another twenty-five years to your sentence. Now let me see. With those other charges, plus this one, that will make a total of seventy-five years in prison. Wow! You'll be almost one hundred years old when you get out. You know what, Vicki, you're going to die in prison!"

Die in prison? How horrible. I had heard they even buried you in a common grave!

Cecelia still couldn't look me in the eye. She kept staring at the floor. But I noticed once when she turned toward one of the detectives, her eyes were all red. She looked as though she hadn't slept in weeks. They must have pressured her to testify against me.

When I finally caught her eye, she said softly, "I'm sorry, Vicki. I mean, I'm really sorry. I warned you. But they said they would take my kids away from me if I didn't testify against you. I couldn't stand that, Vicki. I'm sorry! I'm really sorry!" And she burst into tears.

Detective Forminio took her by the arm and gently led her out of the room. She was sorry; but where did that leave me?

In a few moments, when they returned, I knew these guys were about to work me over. Should I just confess and get it over with?

That's why I was so surprised when Detective Leach said, "Vicki, we want to work a deal with you."

"Deal? What kind of a deal?"

"We're going to let you go free," he said.

Free? I jumped up because I couldn't believe what I was hearing. "Did you say free?" I squealed.

They both nodded. "Yes, that's what we're going to do," Detective Forminio said. "In a few moments you can walk out of here. No seventy-five years in prison."

I studied them. They really were serious. But the whole thing didn't make sense. Were they trying to trick me into a confession and then say they never said anything about letting me go?

"Okay, level with me. What's the deal?"

"All you have to do, Vicki, is help us out."

"What do you mean, help you out?"

"Well," Detective Leach said, "if we're going to be good enough to let you go with all we've got against you, then you'll have to be good enough to help us out—like playing detective."

Then it hit me. They wanted me as a stool pigeon.

"Hey, no way!" I protested. "I mean, no way! I'm no stool pigeon."

"Okay, Vicki, have it your way," Detective Leach said softly. "And your way will be seventy-five years in the slammer. But maybe after a couple of years in there, you'll reconsider."

"Yes," Detective Forminio said, "I guess we're going to have to let her rot in those filthy cells, Bill. It seems a shame."

Both of them turned to walk out. Was this my chance? Was I about to blow it forever? Would I ever get out if I didn't cooperate with them? I didn't know, but I figured I'd better not let them get out. I lunged and grabbed their arms. "Hey, wait!" I exclaimed. "Let's sit down and talk this over again."

They returned to their chairs, and Detective Leach said, "Vicki, we've got you good. But we also have a horrible drug problem on our hands. New Orleans is being destroyed by drug traffic. The mayor has ordered us to stop the flow, and we need all the help we can get. Vicki, we need your help."

Now I was really jammed up against the wall. If I said I would help them, it was the same as admitting my guilt. Somehow I couldn't believe these guys were on the level. They could easily trap me, now. But I had to find out what they had in mind. I wasn't anxious to spend the rest of my life behind bars.

"What do I have to do?"

"Not really all that much. At times we may put a hidden microphone on you to record conversations. Other times we may ask you to keep your eyes open and give us a description of certain people or of their activities. We may ask you to purchase drugs from different people at various locations. Things such as that."

"You have to be kidding!" I exploded. "As soon as someone on the street finds out I'm a stool pigeon, you're going to find my body in some bayou."

"That rarely happens," Detective Leach said. "But may I appeal to your patriotism? Young girls like you are being decimated by drugs. Many murders are committed because of drugs. People's lives are being destroyed; families are being broken up. Doesn't that mean anything to you, Vicki?"

I hadn't really thought about it much one way or the other, and at that time I guess I really didn't care. I knew I was scared to death at the idea of being a stool pigeon. But I was scared to death at the prospect of seventy-five years in prison. So did I really have a choice?

"What about it?" Detective Forminio asked.

I had to come to a decision. They had all the evidence against me, so there was no way I could beat the rap. But if I went along with them, I'd probably get killed—regardless of what they said. But I might get killed in prison, too. I figured it would be better to take my chances on the street.

"Okay, I'll go along. But you guys had better be for real; that's all I've got to say."

"Okay, Vicki, you stay here, and we'll be back in a little while. We'll have to work out a few things with the court."

I sat there alone, sweating it out, wondering how long I would last on the streets.

Then it hit me. Who said I had to go along with them? Once I got out of here, I could give them false information. I could point out the wrong persons. I could really foul them up and be a hero on the streets! All I had to do was to make it look as though I was going along with them. That would keep me out of jail.

But what would happen if they found out what I was doing? Would they bust me, then, and still give me seventy-five years in the slammer?

What choices! Either seventy-five years in the slammer or getting murdered for being a stool pigeon.

I might as well accept my fate. Either way, it wasn't going to be very long before I was dead.

7

When the two detectives returned, they brought a bunch of papers for me to sign. They explained that I was being let out on my own recognizance. The judge and the district attorney's office had worked out a deal that I didn't have to post bail. But there was a big hitch: I would eventually have to come back and face the judge.

Detective Leach explained that my future depended upon how well I behaved out in the street. I was never to get high again, nor was I to be involved directly in the purchase or sale of drugs, unless they arranged it. My primary responsibility was to point out the pushers.

They had me sign a statement that I was not forced into this deal; it was my own choice. I studied that paper carefully. Was there a loophole in it? And what if I decided not to cooperate once I was out?

There were so many legal terms in that paper that I really wasn't sure what I was signing. But all I cared about was being able to get out of this dump.

After I signed all the papers, the two detectives walked me down the hall to the main front door. I was looking out at freedom!

Detective Leach handed me a slip of paper with a telephone number on it. "Your first responsibility, Vicki," he said, "is to call this number at eleven tonight. I'll give you further instructions then."

"Where are you going?" Detective Forminio asked.

That was a good question. I'd probably go to Leon's place, but I didn't dare tell them that. So I said, "I want to go back to where I can live a drug-free life, back to where I was living before I got into trouble—my grandmother's house."

"Are you sure?" Detective Leach asked.

"Of course. Where else would I go?"

"Maybe to someplace like Leon Prout's apartment?" Detective Leach said with a smile.

How in the world did they know about Leon? Had they busted him? I'd better call their bluff.

"Leon Prout?" I asked. "Who in the world is he?"

"Vicki, Vicki," Detective Forminio chided, "I just don't know about you. I thought we could trust you. Maybe we ought to take these papers and rip them up. You're not even on the sidewalk yet, and already we're having trouble with you."

I wasn't about to get this close to freedom and blow it, so I said, "Okay, okay, so I know Leon. But I'm not going to touch him with a ten-foot pole."

They didn't look convinced.

"Come on, you guys, trust me, will you? I am going to my grandmother's house. I'll call you from there tonight."

"No, Vicki, we don't want you going to your grandmother's," Detective Leach said.

"What? What do you want, then? You want me to go to my mother's? She's a real creep, you know. I won't go straight staying with her!"

"No, we've got another place for you," Detective Forminio said.

"Where?"

"Leon Prout's apartment."

"Leon Prout's apartment?" I yelled. "I thought we just

went through all that! For crying out loud, why don't you guys make up your minds?"

"We didn't say you couldn't go there. In fact, it's better if you are somewhere in the French Quarter. All we asked you, Vicki, was whether you knew Leon. Now we're really serious about this project and what you're doing. And we know all about Leon."

I wondered how much they really knew.

"When you were busted in the hospital," Detective Forminio went on, "the detectives could have easily busted Leon at the same time. They knew you two were there together. But they decided to grab you on the false-prescription charge and tail Leon right to his pusher."

This was going to be funny. Leon didn't have a pusher; all he did was knock off drugstores and hospitals. Leon *was* the pusher!

"I don't know how much you know about Leon Prout," Detective Forminio continued, "but we know he's a specialist in picking up girls and then getting them to work for him. The girls get busted, and Leon goes free for lack of evidence. But this time we've got our eyes on Leon."

"You think you know a lot about Leon, don't you?" I shot back. "Okay, I'll level with you about him. Leon's no big-time pusher; he's just a little boy. So we did get drugs and sell a few on the streets. But you know as well as I do we got those drugs through prescriptions—from doctors or hospitals. And that's the truth."

The two laughed. "Yes, that's the truth—but not the whole truth," Detective Leach said. "Leon has a record longer than my arm. His girl before you was Cornelia Lewis. Now that guy Leon is smart. He used Cornelia as his courier. He sold drugs from his apartment, and Cornelia had to run out and get the drugs from his connection. She carted drugs all the time. But one day she double-crossed Leon and sold half the package. He found out about it, and you know what happened next?"

I had heard about situations such as that on the street. And I knew there was only one thing a pusher would do if a courier took half of his drugs. He would kill that person.

"Listen," I said, "I know Leon. He's been kind to everyone."

"Sure, Leon's kind," Detective Leach answered sarcastically. "Tell that to Cornelia. We found her body down in the water near the docks. She had been dead for a week; her body was bloated."

Leon wouldn't do a thing like that, would he? "Hey, you two may know the drug scene," I responded, "but I know a little bit about it, too. She could have been knocked off by a junkie who stole her drugs. Word gets around on the streets about who the couriers are."

"Smart girl, Vicki; smart girl!" Detective Forminio said. "You got my point. When you deal with guys like Leon, you deal with some tough dudes. Now I can't say that Leon killed Cornelia. But we know she cheated him. So whether a junkie knocked her off or Leon knocked her off, we can't say for sure. But she got killed!"

I guess I had been lucky with Leon so far. Would he ever do something like that to me?

"Now why am I telling you all this?" Detective Forminio asked. "Because I want you to keep your eyes open. Watch yourself. I know we really haven't given you much of a choice in this situation; but since you've agreed to work for us, we can't emphasize it enough that you've got to keep your eyes open."

Oh, no! Here I thought I was going to the security of Leon. Then they threw this at me. I knew I was going to be scared to death, no matter what I did or where I was. What a life!

"You guys act like I'm going to get killed," I said. "I mean, I feel like a pig being taken to slaughter. Don't I have any say-so in where I go and what I do?"

"You sure do," Detective Leach answered. "The choice that you've got to make is not to take any drugs and not to sell any drugs. And you be sure to call at eleven every night. Do that, and you stay free. But, baby, if you mess it up, we'll throw the book at you. And you'll be picked up again and you'll rot in jail!"

"Okay, suppose I go to Leon's apartment. What then?"

"When you make your telephone call, make sure he's not around," Detective Leach answered. "Make an excuse about going out for a breath of fresh air, or go down to the drugstore for something. But stay under cover."

"You mean you are sending me out into that jungle, and I'm going to have to go out there without a knife or a gun or anything to protect myself?"

"Well, not quite," Detective Leach said. "Here—take this." He reached inside his jacket and handed me my .357 magnum.

"How in the world did you get that?" I asked in surprise.

"Dr. Walter Webber donated it to the cause of justice," Detective Forminio said with a laugh.

"Come on, you guys. Dr. Webber is a detective, like you. He didn't donate it."

"Well, of course he turned it in as evidence when you got busted. But the district attorney agreed with us that you'd better carry it—just in case."

I'd never heard of cops giving a gun back before, so this really must be serious business.

I hadn't noticed it before, but Detective Forminio had

my purse behind his back, and he chose this moment to hand it back to me. When I unzipped it to put my gun in it, I fumbled through to see what they had taken out and what they had left. The only thing that seemed to be missing was my works. I knew they would keep those as evidence. Besides, I shouldn't need them because I was supposed to stay off drugs. Of course, those false prescriptions were gone, too. I guess they figured the gun really wasn't all that important to their evidence against me. They still had enough to send me off for a long stretch.

"Okay, Vicki, you're free to go now—unless you have some more questions," Detective Leach said. "Just remember to call me tonight at eleven!"

I wasn't about to ask any more questions when I could get out now. One of them opened the door for me, and I walked down the steps and along the sidewalk. I turned to see if the detectives were watching me, but they had already gone inside. So I took a deep breath. Oh, it felt good to be free. But for how long? And at what price?

I hailed a cab to Leon Prout's apartment. I felt strange, walking up to his door and knocking; I usually just walked in. But this time I wasn't sure what to expect.

It was a few moments before the door opened. But there was Leon, a look of absolute surprise on his face when he saw me. "Vicki, what in the world are you doing here?"

I had to begin to learn to lie with a straight face, so I said, "You know I got busted at the hospital. But then the cops suddenly let me go. I didn't have to post bail or anything. I thought it was rather strange but figured maybe it was some legal technicality. You have any idea why they would do that?"

He scratched his head. Then suddenly he grabbed me and jerked me inside, slamming the door and locking all four locks he had put on it since I had been arrested. "Good grief, there is only one reason they would do that, Vicki! They wanted to tail you here so they could bust me!"

"No, no, Leon, I don't think that's true at all. I took a cab over here, and I certainly didn't see anyone tailing me."

Leon ran to the apartment window and looked up the street one way and down the other. Finally he said, "I guess you're right. I sure hope so. But, baby, let me tell you something. They never let you out of jail unless they've got a reason. Let's hope they didn't tail you."

"Wow, Leon, if I had thought that, I sure would have been more careful," I said. "I mean, I could have zigzagged in getting here. I could have taken a bus, then a cab, and then walked. I sure hope I don't get you in any trouble."

He walked over, put both arms around me, and drew me close. "It's all right," he said. "And, Vicki, you don't know how I've missed you and how I've worried about you. I was waiting for you in that hospital when I spotted a detective. I got really nervous and took off running. I jumped in the first cab that came along—that's when I saw they had you."

So that *was* Leon I had spotted in the cab.

"Okay, Leon, but why didn't you come down to the jail? You could have bailed me out. You could have helped me."

"Baby, you don't understand," he remonstrated. "They weren't after you; they were after me! And if I had gotten busted, that would have been the end for both of us. So I was making some calls, trying to get a friend to go down there and bail you out. But that's all behind us, now. You're here!"

Leon had just started to kiss me when a guy walked out of the bedroom. I glanced at him in surprise. Then I yelled, "Josh Perry! What are you doing here?"

Josh and I had gone to high school together. He was the captain of the football team, student-body president—you know the kind—voted most likely to succeed. But what was he doing here?

"Vicki," Josh said, "it's good to see you again. Leon told me about your little hassle with the cops."

"But what are you doing here?" I asked.

"Leon and I have a little deal going. It's going to make us a mint!"

"What kind of a deal?"

"We're into heroin and THC," Leon explained. "We are going to get it from ships that come into port from South America. Vicki, you wouldn't believe the connection we've got. We are really going to be rolling in dough!"

Something in me wanted to scream at Josh, to tell him to get out of here while he could. I had had a crush on him in school because he was a guy with such great potential, and he always was every inch a Southern gentleman. But now he was mixed up in drugs. It made me sick.

"Josh, how long have you been in the business?" I asked.

"Not very long. I started college but had to drop out when my dad died. There wasn't enough money for college, then. In fact, I had to help Mom out for a while. I tried to find a job, but it's hard to get one when you don't have a degree. Well, the other day I just happened to run into Leon. He was a friend of a friend, you know. He and I have just started working today, and I'm really excited about it because there's so much easy money in it."

Instead of my talking Josh out of dealing in drugs, he was beginning to talk me into it. I began to feel that heady appeal of the drug culture again. This was the way I wanted to go in life. Lots of easy money. Dealing and selling—and shooting. In fact, I wanted to get off—right now!

"Hey, Leon," I said, "I've been cooped up in jail. Have you got a set of works and a tab that I can get off?"

"Yeah," Leon responded. "But only one bag. You have to be careful with this stuff. If you're not careful, you can OD real easy."

"Wait a second!" Josh interrupted. "I don't mind working with you, Leon, but I don't know anything about Vicki. She might have cops tailing her. Besides, I have one rule: No getting high. As soon as you get high, you lose your senses and go wrong. That's when people get careless. We have too much riding on this deal to foul up."

"But, Josh," Leon protested, "Vicki's okay. I can vouch for her."

"Well, okay," he answered. Then he looked straight at me. "But, Vicki, if you want me to count you as a partner, you're not to get high!"

"Hey!" I exploded. "What kind of a deal am I getting into? I'm Leon's girl, and I go along with Leon. That makes two against one. So if I want to get high, I get high."

Josh started toward the door, saying, "Fine, but count me out. No way am I going to work with people who get high. I can't afford that kind of a risk."

Leon ran over and grabbed Josh's arm. "Okay, you've got our word; no getting high," he said. "You leave Vicki to me; I'll take care of her."

When I looked offended at that, Leon explained, "Vicki, he's the one who has the connections. I'm nothing without Josh."

So that's the way it was. Well, I'd bide my time.

"Okay, let's finish counting the bags," Josh said. "Your coming in sort of interrupted the process, Vicki."

In the bedroom I spotted quite a number of white cellophane bags on the bed.

"Now, who's the guy you get this stuff from?" I asked as nonchalantly as I could.

"A Colombian freighter comes in here," Leon explained. "The captain is into drugs. So whenever he comes, he brings in a bundle."

"Then you take these bags and sell them on the street?" I asked.

Leon laughed. "No, we don't. We've got people who will come to us, Vicki, and that's the beautiful part of it. They sell it to someone else who sells it to someone else who sells it on the street. We're too high up to play those kind of games, now. I mean, we've got something good going—and it's a lot safer, too."

This was going to be easier than I had thought.

"Tomorrow morning we are to make our first sale," Leon went on. "And, baby, you should see the kind of money we're going to get. Everything you and I have done up to now is kid's stuff!"

As I looked at all those packets of drugs, I just couldn't believe my good luck. A couple of hours ago I was sitting in jail without any hope of ever getting out. Now I was sitting here with a mountain of heroin. But what good was it if I couldn't get off?

Leon and Josh stacked the bags into four piles, wrapped each in brown paper, and tied the package with string and tape. Leon pulled away the rug in a corner of the bedroom. Underneath was a secret trapdoor where he stashed the four packages.

Josh went out for some Kentucky Fried Chicken, and then the three of us sat around watching TV. But I was almost going crazy thinking of all those drugs—and knowing I couldn't get off.

The station break at eleven brought me back to reality. I

was supposed to call Detective Leach. But how could I possibly have known about the terrific deal awaiting me at Leon's apartment? When I thought about all those drugs and all that easy money, I decided that no way was I going to call any detective. I had something too good going here to take a chance on blowing it.

The movie was boring, so Leon suggested we all hit the sack, since we had a big day coming up tomorrow.

It felt great to be sleeping in a real bed again. But somehow I couldn't sleep because I kept thinking about those drugs. If I sneaked out one of those bags and snorted, nobody would ever know. And I'd have enough time to enjoy my high before Leon and Josh got up.

Leon was sound asleep, and I could hear Josh's rhythmic breathing from where he was sleeping in the living room on the sofa. So I eased out of bed, tiptoed over to the corner of the room, pulled back the rug, and lifted the board. *Squeak!* Oh, no! I wheeled around and looked at Leon. He stirred and rolled over, but he didn't wake up.

I took hold of one package, lifted it out of its hiding place, and slowly and quietly unwrapped it. I pulled out a bag, rewrapped the package, and put everything back the way it was. Simple!

Clutching the little packet tightly, I walked into the bathroom and shut the door. Then I sat on the toilet seat, opened the bag of heroin, moved it up next to my nose, and inhaled. The white powder hit my nostrils; the membranes soaked it in; I felt the high. They really did have good stuff.

I lowered the bag to my lap and breathed deeply. This was really good.

I had just started to raise the bag to my nose again when the bathroom door opened. There stood Leon!

8

I thoroughly expected Leon to slap me silly when he caught me sniffing that heroin in the bathroom. After all, he had promised Josh that we would stay clear of the drugs.

But he didn't do that. He didn't cuss me or grab the bag away, either. Instead, he stepped inside and quietly eased the door shut behind him. "Beautiful, Vicki; just beautiful!" he said. "Let me join you."

Leon grabbed the bag and held it up to his nostrils and really inhaled. It hit him, and he reeled back almost like a drunk. Oh, no! He had snorted too much. His eyes started to go back; his knees wobbled. Then he caught himself.

"Take it easy," I cautioned, "or you'll OD."

I grabbed the bag from him and snorted again. Back and forth that little bag went, and soon all the white powder was gone. Both of us were as high as could be.

"Too bad we couldn't shoot up half this stuff," Leon said. "We'd get so high we'd never come down!"

We both laughed at that. Then I began to scratch my nose and arms to get even more sensation.

"Want to try another bag?" I asked.

"Yeah. But let me get this one. If I should get caught, I can make up some excuse about counting them to see for sure how many bags we've got."

I sat there waiting while Leon went for another bag. Dilaudids were all right, but this heroin from Colombia was something else. Too bad I hadn't discovered it before. Up to this time I'd always been afraid of the heroin I could get on the streets. You never knew what you were getting. But being in on a deal like this, where we knew exactly the quality—wow!

In a few minutes Leon was back. He not only had the heroin but also his works. He drilled me first. Then he drilled himself. Then he showed me six more bags in his pocket. "We'll use these to celebrate with tomorrow night," he said, smiling. Good old Leon. I was going to stay with him forever.

He got some tape out of the medicine chest and taped the bags underneath the toilet tank. Then we both crawled back in bed, really enjoying the high.

I guess we finally dozed off because when I opened my eyes, it was light outside. Goodness, it was already ten o'clock! I reached over to awaken Leon, but he was gone. So I jumped up, put on my clothes, and headed for the living room. Leon and Josh were watching TV, so I got myself a cup of coffee and joined them.

When Josh asked if I had slept well, I stole a side glance at Leon and answered, "Anything would beat that bench in jail!"

Then I asked, "What's the schedule for today?"

"We've got to be at the Riverside Motel at exactly noon," Josh said.

"Riverside?" I asked. "Isn't that a pretty fancy place to go to exchange drugs?"

Josh laughed. "I guess, Vicki, we're going to have to give you a few lessons. You always go to the place where the cops would least expect you to be. I suppose you would go down on Bourbon Street and exchange right on the corner where everybody's hanging out, right?"

I didn't answer. Obviously Josh had a point. I certainly

wouldn't think in terms of the swanky hotels as a place to exchange drugs. But it really was a clever idea. I guess if I were going to be involved in big-time drug traffic, I did need to learn some things quickly.

At about eleven Josh herded us all outside to his car. I was in for another surprise. It was a six-year-old Malibu!

I didn't say anything at that moment, but when we started driving, I offered, "Josh, I'm a little surprised at the car."

"Oh?"

"Yeah, well, it's nice enough, I guess. But I expected you—"

"You expected me to be driving a new Cadillac or Lincoln, right?"

"Well, yeah."

"Vicki, you really do have a lot to learn," Josh replied, laughing. "You failed at the idea of where the exchange was to take place. Now about this matter of cars. You don't spend your money on new cars and flashy stuff like that. Why, if I drove a Rolls Royce, some cop would pull me over and ask what I do for a living. Then I'd have to start lying—and maybe he'd pull me in on suspicion, or get a warrant and search my car or my apartment. Fancy cars stick out too much. All you need is a plain, little car—one that's like a lot of other plain, little cars, one that can easily get lost in the crowd."

I was beginning to feel more and more secure in this deal. This Josh was a brain.

I noticed we weren't taking a straight shot to the motel—but I figured that one out by myself. He wanted to double back and go around here and there to be sure we weren't being tailed. But that kind of driving did bring another revelation.

All three of us were seated in the front—and it was a little crowded. I was in the middle, of course. And with Josh doing a lot of stop-and-go driving, every once in a while his ankle would brush up against my leg. At first I thought he must have had a broken bone from playing football. But that didn't make sense, so I asked, "Josh, what's that on your ankle?"

He reached down. Suddenly, in his hand was a small pistol. "That's where I carry it, baby."

"That's not the only place, either," Leon added.

Josh put the pistol back in his leg holster and then showed me another one inside his coat.

"Why two guns?" I asked.

"Vicki, that should be obvious," Josh said, laughing again. Suppose we get stopped, and I'm frisked. First thing they do is go for your chest, right? Okay, they find that gun and pull it out. But ninety percent of the time those dumb cops stop there. So when they're not watching, you can get to the other one and get the drop on them. Same thing when you get into a fight. If a guy gets the best of you and gets your gun away, you've still got your reserve on your leg. Two guns are always better than one when—"

"Hey!" I interrupted. "I saw something like that on TV. A lot of detectives carry two guns. Did you see that on TV?"

As soon as I said the word *detective,* I felt Josh stiffen. "Hey, what's the matter?" I asked. "You afraid of detectives?"

"You'd better believe I am," he replied. "Detectives will bust you, and bust you good. Don't mention that word anymore when we're on a delivery. It's bad luck. Besides, it makes me nervous."

"Okay, okay," I said. "But you sure are a great teacher, Josh."

He grinned that little-boy grin that let me know he was pleased with what I had said.

We had been driving around for about thirty minutes when Josh pulled to the curb and said, "Okay, everybody out."

I thought it was strange, but Leon didn't ask any questions, so neither did I. When we were all standing on the curb, Josh said, "Okay, Vicki, this is where we leave you."

"Hey, what's the deal? We're at least five miles from Riverside," I remonstrated. "What do you mean, you're going to leave me here?"

"Vicki, there's a nice restaurant over across the street. Go in there and buy yourself a good lunch. In about an hour or so, we'll come by and join you. And then we can all celebrate."

"Now, wait a minute—" I started.

"I'm sorry, Vicki, but I just can't take you with us," Josh interrupted. "I don't think you ought to go with us because something might happen. We may have to do our thing, and I couldn't stand to see you get hurt. You know, we were good buddies in school, and I care enough about you that I don't want to see anything happen to you. So please, just wait in that restaurant over there. Get yourself some luscious dessert to celebrate getting out of jail. Then Leon and I will be back soon—right after the sale."

"Now wait a minute!" I protested. "I thought I was in on this deal. You're sounding like a male chauvinist, Josh. I can handle myself in any shoot-out. I think this drug business has gone to your head and scrambled your brains. I'm a full partner in this. Right, Leon?"

I looked at him for support. So far he hadn't said a word. Would he stand by me now?

"Come on, Josh," he finally said, "let Vicki come with us. We can trust her. Besides, we might need her."

I unzipped my purse and pulled out my .357 magnum. "Josh, I don't know whether I have to prove to you how good a shot I am. See that light over across the street?" I aimed.

Josh quickly reached toward the gun and aimed it at the sidewalk. "Put that thing away, Vicki. Somebody could see us and report it to the police. We sure don't need that right now."

I jerked away and pointed the gun right at him. "What I am trying to say, Josh, is this: Let's all three of us get back in that car and drive to the Riverside Motel. I would hate to use this gun. I mean, I would really hate to use it on you. But I will if you try to keep me out of this deal. Then Leon and I could collect on the whole thing for ourselves!"

"Vicki, I wish you would listen to reason," Josh pleaded. "I am just saying all of this for your own good. Please wait in the restaurant. We'll be right back; I promise. You can trust me."

I cocked the gun. "I'm not kidding," I threatened.

He threw up his hands in frustration. "Okay, okay, but don't say I didn't try to warn you. And put that gun away. Now!"

I released the safety catch, stuffed the gun back into my purse, and the three of us took off for the motel. This time as we drove along, no one said anything. But I was wondering if I could really trust Josh—or would he keep trying to cut me out? After all, it would be better for him to divide the loot two ways rather than three. I guess he really stood to gain nothing from my being a partner.

We arrived at the motel with about twenty minutes to spare. Leon carried the drugs in a thick attaché case. I was about to ask where the exchange would take place when Josh said, "Okay, we're already checked into room 501. I've rented the room for a month and have the key right here."

I couldn't get over the beautiful lobby—four stories high with waterfalls and lush tropical plants. It was a real paradise. I wondered why we couldn't spend the month here—since Josh had already paid for it, anyway. It sure beat Leon's apartment.

The elevator took us quickly and quietly to the fifth floor. Josh pointed to the right, and we went to the end of the hall. He opened the door to 501 and motioned us inside.

My eyes quickly took in everything. This was a beautiful corner room with half of the walls in glass. What plush luxury!

"Wow, Josh! What did you have to pay for this for a month?"

"Plenty!" he replied. "Plenty!"

I sank into an easy chair and looked at my watch. Fifteen minutes to go. Then, as I kept studying the layout of the place, I wondered why Josh would pick a room like this. There was no way to escape except down that hall. If for some reason we did get busted by the cops and were on the first floor, we would have a chance to jump for it. But not here. It would be suicide to jump from the fifth floor. Maybe Josh wasn't so smart, after all.

I started to say something about it, but Josh and Leon were both nervously pacing the floor. Besides, Josh had warned me not to bring up anything about detectives. So I shut up, but I worried.

I glanced at my watch every minute or so. The attaché

case rested on the coffee table. I started thinking about the riches the contents of that little case were about to bring us.

Sure enough, right at twelve, straight up, someone knocked lightly on our door. I jumped out of the chair. Josh and Leon exchanged nervous glances.

"Okay," Josh said—and he still seemed to be in control of the operation—"I want all three of us to go to the door together—just in case this is some kind of a setup."

I nodded, but I made sure both of them were in front of me.

Josh looked through the peephole in the door. Then he turned to us and, smiling broadly, announced, "It's them. We're in luck!"

He jerked the door open. Then everything broke loose as six huge guys rushed us. Before I could even think of going for my gun, I was slammed against the wall. I wasn't sure what kind of guys they were until I felt the handcuffs. Cops!

I glanced over. They had Leon cuffed already, too. But where was Josh? Did he push by them and get away?

Then I spotted him out in the hall. He had both guns in his hands, and they were aimed into the room. He had gotten by them. Now maybe he could get them to let us go. "Pull the trigger, Josh!" I called. "Don't be afraid."

But the stupid guy just stood there and smiled. And the cops didn't seem to be paying any attention to him.

One of the cops pulled out a badge and told us we were under arrest for sales and possession. I couldn't believe it. We had been set up!

But why hadn't they touched Josh? Anticipating my un-asked question, he came back into the room, put his guns back into their holsters, reached inside his coat, and flipped out a badge. "Sorry, Vicki," he said, "but I tried to warn you not to come. What else can I say?"

That Josh was an undercover narcotics agent! He must have been after Leon. And they got me in the bargain!

Another detective read us our rights. Then they took Leon out. When they did, Josh came over and said, "Vicki, how I wish you had gotten out of that car when I asked you to. I was trying to let you know about me. I tried to lay a hint last night about the drugs. I really didn't want to see you hurt this way."

Why was Josh so concerned about me? He had always been decent to me, but he sure never had indicated anything more than he thought I was a nice girl.

"I know all about your case, Vicki," he went on. "I work with Detectives Leach and Forminio. I was even waiting for you to make an excuse to call them last night. But you didn't even make an effort. And I sure couldn't say anything that would tip off Leon. We had put too much effort into nabbing him. I guess I'm also disappointed, Vicki. We still have a lot of undercover work to do to try to dry up this drug traffic. The three of us were really counting on you to help us. We knew we'd soon have Leon out of the way. You could still have used the apartment and had a good base to work from in the Quarter. But now you've blown the whole thing!"

Suddenly it hit me how stupid I'd been. I'd been given a real chance, and I hadn't even made it through twenty-four hours! A little tear started to trickle down my cheek, and I bit my lip to keep from breaking down completely.

Josh gently took my arm and lifted me up. "Now what?" I asked.

"Back to jail, Vicki. We've got no choice."

I guess I knew that. I just didn't want to admit it. Once again I was facing a sentence of seventy-five years. Oh, no!

It would be even more now with these new charges!

The first two guys I ran into at the jail were Detectives Leach and Forminio. They didn't say anything—just shook their heads in disbelief. I guess they really had trusted me.

After I was booked, a matron led me back to that same dismal cell. I sat on that hard bench and buried my head in my hands. I was alone now, but no tears would come. In just twenty-four hours I had completely blown my opportunity for freedom. I was so angry, so confused, so frustrated, so hopeless. Would I ever again have a chance to be free? Or would bars confine me for the rest of my days?

I don't know how long I sat there, but I heard the cell door down at the far end of the hall unlock. I raised my head slightly and saw a matron coming.

She unlocked my cell and announced coldly, "A couple of detectives want to talk to you."

I didn't answer—just sat there with my elbows on my legs—so she walked over and grabbed my arm roughly.

"Get your hands off me, you creep!" I snarled.

She backed off. "Listen, kid, I understand how you feel. You got out and got busted again. Hey, that's nothing. It happens to prostitutes all the time. You'll get over it."

She grabbed me again and started to yank me to my feet. I pushed her away, yelling, "I told you, get your hands off me. I don't want to talk to anybody. Not you, not any stupid detectives, not the mayor, not the chief of police. Nobody! I just want to sit here and think for a little while."

"Say, you're kind of sassy for a girl in jail, aren't you? One of the things you'd better learn, honey, is that in jail you don't have any rights. If some detectives want to talk to you, then you're going to talk. Here, I'm the one who tells you what you can and can't do. And right now I'm telling you to get up off your rear end and come with me.

Now you get up before I make you do it!"

She grabbed my arm again and yanked. But she had to have both of her feet firmly planted on the floor to do that. So I lifted one foot as though I were going to get up. Then I came down as hard as I could with my heel on her toe.

You should have heard the eruption! She immediately let go of me and started dancing around that cell on one foot, screaming and cursing.

Her antics were so funny I started to laugh. Well, that did it! "You'll pay for this, kid!" she screamed as she rubbed her toe. "Nobody does something like that to old Nellie and gets by with it!"

"Oh, calm down; you'll get used to it, Nellie," I replied with all the sarcasm I could muster. "You know how it is. A prisoner gets a little upset over being busted and takes it out on the matron. I'm sure it's happened before. And it'll probably happen again. As I say, you'll get used to it."

The matron gingerly put her sore foot on the floor and wagged her finger at me. "Okay, you get up off that bench before I jerk you up by the roots of your peroxide blonde hair!"

Would she dare? I knew I wouldn't sit still for that kind of treatment. I spat on the floor—I guess it was a kind of a dare to her—and just sat there. I didn't even look at her.

"Listen, you little punk," she screamed again, "you must think I'm kidding. You stand up this instant, or I'll make you do it. And you'll be real sorry if I have to do that!"

I gritted my teeth and waited. If she tried to lay a hand on my hair, I was going to knock her flat!

"Get up! I said, get up!"

As she headed for me again, I watched her feet. This time I was going to get the other one. That would really put her out of commission.

"Get up before I knock you silly!" she screamed.

Her feet were right in front of me, now. I raised my foot and stomped again. But this time she was expecting it and pulled her feet out of the way. My foot came down hard on the cement floor—and that hurt. But I also realized that while she was sidestepping my foot, she had grabbed my hair and was yanking me upward! It felt as if someone had stuck a million needles in my scalp.

I flew upward involuntarily. But as I did, I saw her snarling face in front of mine. I tightened my fist and hit her nose full force.

She screamed bloody murder, spun me around, and kicked my feet out from under me. She pounced on me like a tiger pouncing on its prey, got my hands behind my back, whipped out her handcuffs, and clamped them on me. Then I was on the floor, face down. She stood up, pushed her foot down hard on my head, squashing my nose against the cement. Oh, it hurt! Then she tromped her foot down again, screaming, "I ought to kick out your brain from your empty little head! You're a punk—nothing but a no-good punk!"

She grabbed my hair again and forced me to my feet. I tried to kick, but her grip was too strong, and the pain was killing me.

Spinning me around, she grabbed the front of my blouse and pushed a fist up into my face. That's when I first saw that her nose was all bloody. I had really scored with that one punch!

"You're lucky, kid, real lucky!" she growled. "The last time someone tried to handle old Nellie, they had to take her to the emergency room. The doctors worked six hours trying to fix her up. I busted her ribs. I busted her nose. And I almost busted her legs. Now, baby, one more false move, and you're heading for the emergency room with all sorts of problems that you don't have yet. You understand?"

The handcuffs kept me from pasting her another one right in her big mouth. I didn't care if I had to go to the hospital. I didn't care whether I lived or died. But no way was any matron going to pull my hair like that and get by with it. I'd get even with old Nellie!

Still pulling me by the hair, she forced me out the cell door and started pushing me down the hall. I stiffened my legs, and she stopped pushing. She even let go of my hair. I turned around to see what was going on. Just as I did, I saw it coming—but not soon enough to do anything about it. Her foot was heading for the seat of my pants! Too late! I couldn't move that fast. That foot really struck me and sent me reeling down the hall.

"You're not getting by with this!" I screamed as I fell against the wall. I wheeled around, raising my foot to let her have it right where it hurt. But as I kicked, she grabbed my leg and then kicked my other leg out from underneath me. The handcuffs kept me from balancing myself, and I went crashing to the cement floor. I saw stars. Then everything went black.

9

When I finally opened my eyes again, my vision was blurry. But I could make out the faces of two cops.

"Hey, little girl," one of them said, "you're really mad at the world, aren't you?"

I didn't know whether to spit in his face or admit defeat. I looked around for the matron, but I couldn't see her anywhere.

"Okay," one of them said, "let's get going now." They lifted me up by my shoulders and started walking down the hall.

"Where is that dirty, filthy woman?" I demanded. "I'm not through with her yet."

One of them laughed. "You mean old Nellie? They had to take her to the emergency room. I think you broke her nose."

A smile flitted across my face. She was the one going to the hospital this time!

"Listen, Nellie Jimenez is the toughest matron in town," the other officer said. "Never pick on her. She won't forget it." Then he laughed.

"I'll never forget it, either," I said. "You'd better keep me away from her, or there's going to be—"

"Listen, kid, I'll tell you something, if you won't quote me," the first officer said. "I, for one, was glad to see old Nellie with a broken nose. It's about time somebody smacked her. She's got a big mouth and gets rough with everybody. She seems to bring out the worst in the prisoners here. In fact, when they took her out of here, some people started cheering. You're probably a heroine."

Inwardly I felt a kind of pride that I hadn't let her get by with that nonsense. But what would happen the next time we met? She would have it in for me—and there wasn't much I could do to her.

My head was throbbing like crazy from the pain of the fall. Oh, how I wanted to reach up and rub it. But there was no way I could do that in handcuffs.

"Hey, can you take these handcuffs off me?" I asked.

They both laughed. "Listen, kid, if we did that, you'd probably knock both of us cold. Besides, it's against regulations. You're now classified as a violent prisoner."

"Me, violent?" I asked. "Take a look. Here I am, five feet two; I weigh one hundred ten pounds. Me, violent? You have to be kidding!"

"Well, just come along with us. A couple of detectives want to talk to you. They can decide about the handcuffs."

They grabbed my arms and started pulling me along again. I wanted to scream, to tell them to get their hands off me. But then I realized there was no sense in fighting these guys; I was their heroine!

They took me through the outer, locked gate and to a room where Detectives Leach and Forminio were waiting. They made me stand there in front of them.

"Well, well, if it isn't Little Miss Muffett again," Detective Leach started in. "We gave you a chance, baby; but this time you're in jail for good. Probably for life!"

I was hurting, but his attitude infuriated me. "Okay , let's cut the small talk," I said. "I've been set up, and you know it. Josh Perry, my so-called good friend, somebody I've always admired, did me in. I'm waiting to get into court because I want to testify against that guy. I was set up, and you guys know it!"

"Hey, Vicki, simmer down," Detective Forminio counseled. "Josh is our buddy, too. He told us he did everything he could to stop you from going with them. Now I know you're mad and upset and hurting, and I don't blame you. But don't vent your anger against Detective Perry. Josh is a great guy. He's one of our best undercover agents. You should have listened to him. You've got only one person to blame for your troubles: Vicki Hensley."

I knew that. I knew I should have listened to Josh. But it was too late now, and I was heading for prison.

"Listen, you guys," I said, "please let me sit down. And please take these cuffs off me. I promise I won't try a thing with you two. But I'm really feeling woozy from that little altercation out there."

"Yeah, we heard about that. That kind of behavior won't help you any, Vicki."

"Come on; don't preach at me."

Detective Leach took off the handcuffs and helped me into a chair. "Comfortable?" he asked. I nodded.

"Okay, then," he went on, "what's your sex life like?"

I bolted upright in the chair. "Sex life? What business is that of yours?"

Don't tell me these two detectives were going to try to get fresh with me! Besides, that question embarrassed me. It wasn't the kind of thing I talked about.

I settled back and stared at the ceiling, so Detective Leach repeated, "How's your sex life?"

I kept staring at the ceiling, but I was raging inside. First I got beat up by the matron. Now I was being humiliated by these two detectives.

When he kept badgering me, I finally answered, "I'm pregnant."

Detective Forminio, looking very surprised, got up and walked over to me. Leaning in toward me, he asked, "You're pregnant? How do you know?"

Typical man! "Listen, stupid, don't you think a girl knows when she is pregnant?"

Leach looked at Forminio. I knew I had them, so I decided to make this into a really big story.

"Well, I'll tell you how I know I'm pregnant. First of all, I got weak and went to bed with a man. And the second thing, I've missed my period for three months, now. I suggest you take me to a doctor, because when it gets into the paper about how one of your matrons beat up a pregnant inmate, everybody in this police department is going to be in big trouble!"

"Sure, sure!" Detective Forminio laughed.

"All right, you guys, I'm warning you. That matron jerked me by my hair and threw me to the cement floor. She didn't do it once; she did it many times. She stomped on my head. She stomped on my stomach. She probably killed the child I'm carrying. I told her I was in pain, but she wouldn't stop hitting me. So help me, if I miscarry, I'll blame that matron for the murder of my child!"

"And who is the father?" Detective Forminio asked, ignoring my threats.

"I was just coming to that," I said, "and you two dudes had better brace yourselves for this one. Three months ago I was out on the street minding my own business when Josh Perry came up and started talking. One thing led to another, and I invited him up to my room. He's the father of my baby!"

I watched to see how these guys would respond to that revelation. They looked at each other in surprise, then Detective Leach said, "Just a minute. Let me check on something."

Detective Forminio sat there looking pretty nervous. Maybe they had gone beyond the bounds of the law. Maybe they would have to let me go. I knew that happened sometimes to other prisoners—they had to let them go on some technicality of the law.

Moments later, when the office door opened, there stood Detective Leach with Josh Perry. They both sat down.

"Josh," Detective Leach began, "we thought you ought to know that Vicki Hensley has implicated you as the father of her unborn baby."

"What?" Josh yelled in surprise. "I did what?"

"Listen, Josh," I said, "there's no point in telling lies about it. I know it comes as a surprise to you now; but you know what happened three months ago when you were in my room."

"Let's see," Josh started, "three months ago. That would be about May 16. You claim it was May 16 I went to bed with you?"

"I don't remember the exact day," I said cagily. "But it was around then."

Then the three of them laughed uproariously.

"What's so funny?" I demanded.

When they ignored me and kept laughing, I yelled, "Listen, you three filthy detectives. You're probably all sex fiends. You've probably all been to bed with all kinds of women. Maybe you even make the women prisoners here bow to your demands. And, Josh, you may try to keep up that snow-white image of yours, but you know I'm telling the truth!"

They kept laughing, so I demanded again, "What's so funny?"

"Vicki," Detective Forminio said, "I don't know whether to love you or hit you. You're a girl with such great potential, but you keep getting yourself into more and more trouble. Don't you know that an accusation like this in court will not be taken lightly by the judge? Because of the publicity surrounding things like this, the judge will order an investigation. Now I don't know whether you're planning to testify against Josh in court or not. But for your own good, I would suggest you keep your mouth shut!"

Aha! Now I had these detectives really scared. They were trying to frighten me into keeping my mouth shut. Well, no way was I going to do that—if this could get me out of jail.

"Okay, I know I'm going to be arraigned," I said, "and at that time I'll sing. I'll get that matron. And I'll get Josh. They're both in real trouble."

"And I suppose you want to make a deal with us so you won't tell the judge about Josh, right?" Detective Forminio asked.

"What kind of a deal?"

They were coming my way, now!

"Vicki, there can be no deal," Detective Leach said. "Absolutely no deal. You had your chance."

"Okay, if that's the way you want it," I said. "But you just listen to my beautiful song when I get in there in front of that judge. I'm really going to put the finger on Josh Perry, and he's going to be in trouble for this one!"

Detective Leach walked over to me again. "Vicki, there's something about you that we really like," he started in. "And that's why Joe was trying to tell you to keep your mouth shut. Don't you understand?"

I looked at him quizzically.

"Last May Josh Perry was in France as part of a special investigation unit working with Interpol. Josh couldn't possibly be the father of your baby."

I had to think quick. "Listen, it was probably late April. I can't remember the exact date."

"Too bad, Vicki. He was over there from February until he got back about two weeks ago. Sorry."

I slowly sank back into the chair. "That's why we're saying you'd better keep your mouth shut about this," Detective Forminio said. "It won't take much of an investigation to prove that you're lying—and then that will go on your record, too. Everything like this is just making your case that much harder. Now why don't you just get rid of all that anger you've got bottled up inside you and start doing something positive with your life?"

I bowed my head and stared at the floor. Detective Leach, still standing by me, put his hand on my shoulder and asked softly, "You're not pregnant, are you?"

I shook my head.

For the next few minutes the silence in that room was deafening. It's hard to describe what happened to me next. It seemed as though all the anger drained out of me as I thought of my life and what a terrible mess I'd made of things.

Josh broke the silence when he put his hand on my shoulder and said, "Vicki, I can't help but think of when you and I were in high school and the fun we had. You were such a beautiful girl then—so vivacious and full of life. I knew about the problem with your mom and how you lived with your grandmother and how hard life must have been for you. But during those days you had a tender heart. Now that heart has turned to steel."

I nodded as I remembered, too.

"Two things are likely to happen now, Vicki," he went on. "You're either going to get killed out in the street, or you're going to die in prison. Why don't you give up? Why don't you give yourself the chance to do right?"

I didn't answer. I couldn't. My heart seemed to jump into my throat. Tears formed and trickled down my cheeks.

I looked up at this wonderful young man. Why couldn't we have fallen in love in high school? Things would be so different now if I could be the wife of a man like Josh. But it hadn't happened. And now it was too late.

"You know you'll probably spend a long time in prison," Josh said quietly. "But I know Someone who will go to prison with you. That Someone is Jesus."

Jesus? Don't tell me Josh had become a religious nut! I glanced at the other two detectives to see their reaction. They were standing there smiling and nodding.

"Hey, what's going on here?" I asked. "Did I get locked up in church? Are you guys preaching at me?"

"Well, I certainly don't intend to be preaching," Josh replied, "but all three of us have experienced a tremendous change in our lives. We are all born-again Christians."

"You are what kind of Christians?"

"Born again. Jesus Christ has come into our lives and has given us peace in this troubled world. You know, being detectives, we could easily become cynical because of the problems of injustice and crime and rip-offs and all that sort of thing. But we're police officers with our heads screwed on right because we've discovered that Jesus forgives our sins and helps us to find God's will for our lives. It's the only way to be really happy."

I couldn't believe what I was hearing. In fact, I really

couldn't understand it, either. I'd never had much to do with any kind of religion. Religious people had always impressed me as phonies.

"We're members of an organization known as Cops for Christ," Detective Leach added. "It's an international organization in which police officers have bound themselves together to proclaim the Good News of Christ throughout the world. And in His own way the Lord uses us to minister to people in need."

The other two nodded in agreement. Then Josh looked me square in the eyes and said, "Vicki, Jesus Christ wants to bring you great peace, too. Even if you should end up in prison—as you likely will—you'll discover that if you know Jesus, you may be in prison, but the prison won't be in you."

Prison I understood, and I feared it. I figured I would never survive the system. But all this talk about Jesus—that was something so far removed from my world that I couldn't even begin to understand it.

"We also work with an organization in New York called the Walter Hoving Home," Detective Forminio added. "They've got a terrific program for girls like you—girls who have messed up their lives because of drugs or alcohol or other problems. In fact, girls who come out of prisons and jails go there for help. Some come off the street. Some are sent there by the courts. The important thing is that they do a fantastic job of helping the girls who come to them."

"Don't talk to me about any rehabilitation programs," I said. "I've heard enough about the problems of those places."

"Well, this one isn't a rehabilitation home," Detective Forminio answered. "It's a home for Christian growth. And don't let that term bother you. Up there they teach girls what life is all about and how to really live. They use the Bible because it has some great truths for all of us. It might be the answer for you."

"I knew a girl there—Winnie Gerdon," Josh said. "I worked in Pennsylvania for a short time and heard about her case and later met her. She went through the program at the home. But the charges against her came through, and she was sentenced to serve time in a federal penitentiary. You may not believe this, but while Winnie was serving that term, she stayed true to the Lord. More than that, she used the opportunity of being in prison to share the Gospel with the girls there. They might not have had a chance to hear about Jesus if Winnie hadn't had to serve that prison term. Anyway, she even started her own chapel services for the girls. She had such a beautiful spirit that the prison officials themselves appealed to the judge to reduce her sentence! She had to serve only nine months of her sentence. Today she's married and has two beautiful children. God has been good to her." He paused to be sure I was taking it all in. "Vicki, the Lord wants to do wonderful things in your life, too. As I said, you'll probably go to prison for a long time. But Jesus wants to go with you."

My head was spinning. How could three detectives be talking to me about Jesus? I thought that only preachers talked about religion.

"Vicki," Detective Forminio said, "please forgive us for asking about your sex life. Honestly, we don't really want to know. But this is a standard procedure that we use. You see, we need to get you really mad. After you've blown your stack, it's much easier for us to talk with you rationally. When you came in here after that altercation with Nellie, we knew you were mad at the world and especially at yourself. Somehow we had to get you to release that anger. And that question we asked is one we've learned to use with girls like you. It worked, didn't it? You exploded. But now we've got you calmed down. We couldn't take you before the judge so angry. We sure don't want any outbursts in court—that wouldn't have helped you, either. We got all those false charges out of your system here so you wouldn't be tempted to use them before the judge and hurt yourself even more. So please forgive us."

I couldn't get over the compassion I sensed as he asked me to forgive them. And yet I was still suspicious of anything the cops did. Were they treating me this way to set me up for something else? After all, Josh had set me up before. I'd better keep my head about me. But right now they really seemed concerned about what was likely to happen to me. It seemed strange—and rather comforting—to think that maybe somebody cared about me.

Later, as I stood before the judge at my arraignment, I nervously wondered what was going to happen now. First he fumbled through some papers—probably the record of my previous arrest. Then he looked at me—the kind of a look that goes right through you and you feel as though he can read your innermost thoughts and fears. Maybe he knew I never would amount to anything—that I just didn't have enough strength of character to resist the lure of drugs and easy money. And if he knew that, then this was going to be the beginning of the end. I'd probably be placed behind bars—and stay there forever!

10

I listened listlessly as the district attorney read off the charges: sales, possession, resisting arrest. I felt trapped because I knew they had me.

Then the judge asked me how I wanted to plead. I guess because I still hoped there would be some way out—maybe even plea bargaining again—I blurted out, "Not guilty, your honor."

He set my bail at twenty-one thousand dollars. No way could I or any of my friends or relatives touch that. That meant they'd hold me in jail until my trial. After the trial? Probably seventy-five years in prison. So what was a few weeks in prison before trial?

It didn't take me long to learn the answer to that. The following morning they transferred me to a place called the stockade—it was a prison for women who were awaiting trial. I was told I would be there for several months until my case came up.

Life in the stockade was a real hassle from morning till night—and frequently at night, too.

There was really nothing worth getting up for, but we had to get up at six every morning for breakfast—whether we wanted to eat or not.

After breakfast we had to clean our rooms. (There were ordinarily two girls to a room, but at that time I had a room to myself.) The rooms didn't have any doors—so there wasn't that much privacy. The windows, of course, were barred—and so filthy you could hardly see out of them.

You couldn't get dressed in your cell. You had to wear a bathrobe to the bathroom and take your clothes with you and get dressed there. The clothes, of course, weren't your clothes. You had a prison uniform to wear.

I was told that you couldn't dress in your room because of the lesbians. Of course, there was always a lineup in the bathroom.

After we had cleaned our rooms we were assigned to duties—working in the offices, the laundry, kitchen, and so on.

I quickly learned that the worst thing about jails is not the facility, but that your personal rights are taken away. In fact, you had no rights at all. You did what you were told to do.

Besides the prison system of authority, the women prisoners had their own system. Sometimes they became so powerful that they also controlled the prison system! And if you didn't do what they told you to do, they'd try to kill you. I learned about that the hard way.

Since I was one of the newest ones at the prison, I was assigned the duty that everybody tried to avoid—cleaning the bathrooms. It was bad enough at best, but after I had been doing it for a couple of weeks, I noticed that some of the girls never bothered to flush the toilets after they used them. I thought they were doing it as a point of rebellion. But did it ever stink—and I was the one who really had the problem with it. It didn't seem to bother the prison authorities. They didn't have to clean the johns!

One morning after breakfast, I started to my work assignment, stopping to get the mop and bucket on the way. Before I even walked into the bathroom, I knew I was in trouble. It stunk like you wouldn't believe.

The first toilet was filthy enough to make me gag. I flushed it. The second one was even worse. So was the third one. I almost vomited from the stench.

I flushed each of those, but I told myself that if the fourth one was like this, I was going to find out who was behind this rebellion and try to talk some sense into their heads. This nonsense wasn't hurting the prison authorities. It was just making the whole area worse for us prisoners.

I guess that's when it dawned on me that maybe this wasn't a rebellion against the prison system. Maybe somebody was trying to get at me! All the girls knew who had to clean out the bathrooms!

Sure enough, the fourth toilet was worse than the others. I flushed it quickly and wheeled around and headed out into the hall where some of the other girls were pushing brooms around, supposedly working. When they saw me, they all began to laugh.

Daisy Mae seemed to be laughing the loudest. I couldn't stand that woman, anyway. She was overweight, overbearing, obnoxious, and ugly. I had suspected she was probably a lesbian. Could she be the one behind this whole rebellion?

"Okay, Daisy Mae," I demanded, "what's so funny?"

"What's the matter, Vicki?" she cooed. "We girls heard that you used to live on a farm, and we wanted to make you feel at home. Don't you know we're all a bunch of animals here? Baby, cleaning out those bathrooms is just like cleaning up the stables."

The other girls thought that was hilarious and joined her in uproarious laughter—at my expense.

"Who's the smart one who decided that nobody should flush the toilets?" I demanded.

"Oh, that," Daisy Mae cooed. "I'm sorry, Vicki, but I've

been constipated for two weeks, and I finally got them to give me a laxative. I did all that. You can just be thankful I didn't explode before I got to the toilets. I was so sick when I got through that I just forgot."

I threw the mop down and grabbed Daisy Mae by her blouse. Pulling her up close I snarled, "So help me, if I go back to clean that bathroom tomorrow and those toilets aren't flushed, I'm wrapping that mop around your neck."

She jerked herself away and bellowed, "I dare you!"

The other girls quickly encircled us. One of them yelled, "Ram that mop down her throat, Daisy Mae, and clean out all her stuffings!"

The rest of the girls cackled. Nobody seemed to be on my side, but I didn't care. No way was I going to put up with nonsense like this.

I grabbed Daisy Mae's blouse again and growled in my gruffest voice, "You heard what I said. Don't make me do something I don't want to do. Just remember, I'll be checking those toilets tomorrow morning, and I'll hold you responsible!" With that I relaxed my grip and pushed her back.

She turned to the other girls and said, "Hey, this kid sounds like she wants to take over the prison! Who does she think she is, anyway? She's giving orders like the warden!"

"Hit her, Daisy Mae!" one of them yelled. "Don't take any guff from her!"

Daisy Mae stayed at a distance. But she looked straight at me and said, "Kid, you've got a lot to learn. You've got to know where the power is. And let me tell you something right now: You don't have any power!"

She stepped forward and shoved me. That did it. I grabbed the mop and raised it over my head to let her have it. But just then a matron came running down the hall yelling, "Vicki Hensley, you drop that mop, or you'll be spending a week in solitary!"

That matron was big and ugly, and I knew I didn't have a chance against her. So I lowered the mop.

"Now, what's going on here?" she demanded. "Why aren't you girls at your work stations?"

Should I tell her about the toilets? No, I wouldn't go that route. The rest of the prisoners would never respect me if I did that. I'd always be looked upon as a stool pigeon.

"I was just showing the girls how to do some exercises," I said. "You see, you take something like this mop, raise it above your head, and strengthen your muscles."

"Don't get funny," the matron snapped. "I saw what was happening."

"Hey, matron, no problem; no problem whatsoever. Right, girls?" I turned toward the girls, and they nodded in agreement. So did Daisy Mae. So the matron turned and walked off.

When she was gone, I started back to the bathroom. But over my shoulder I called to Daisy Mae, "Don't forget what I said!"

She started to cuss me out. I felt like turning and wrapping the mop handle around her neck, but the matron had turned and was watching. I knew I'd better cool it.

The rest of that day I noticed most people keeping their distance from me. I knew what they were thinking—that tomorrow morning was going to be the showdown!

Sure enough, next morning the bathroom stunk worse than ever. The first toilet was absolutely filthy. Only this time somebody had also thrown a roll of toilet paper in on top of the mess. If I flushed the toilet, that roll of toilet paper would stop up the plumbing, and the mess would flood all over the floor. Then I would really have something to clean up. But the alternative of reaching into that mess and pulling out that filthy roll of toilet paper was more than my stomach could handle.

So I didn't do anything. I went to the second toilet. It was the same. So was the third, and so was the fourth. Somebody had deliberately thrown toilet paper on top of the filthy mess in each one. This was not rebellion against the authorities. They were out to get at me! Daisy Mae was daring me!

I grabbed my mop, wheeled around, and stomped down the hall looking for her. I didn't have far to go. She was standing right outside the bathroom, feet apart, waiting for me. And so were the rest of the girls.

Instead of going up to her, I turned and went back into the bathroom. I knew she thought I had chickened out. But I had another plan.

Back in the bathroom I took a bucket and dipped filth and those rolls of toilet paper out of the toilets until I had a bucketful. Then, bucket in hand, I returned to the hallway and Daisy Mae.

"I dare you, Vicki," she roared.

She shouldn't have said that. For without a word I swung the bucket and let its contents fly. All that filthy, stinking stuff landed right on target. You should have heard the fuming and sputtering and cursing. I know she didn't think I would ever do it.

Before she could regain herself and start after me, the matrons came running down the hall. They got to her first and slapped handcuffs on her. I didn't see how they could stand to touch her and get into all that stinking, filthy stuff which covered her. And, as I expected, one of them ran over and slapped handcuffs on me, too.

"Just a minute! Just a minute!" I yelled. "Let me explain!"

"You can do your explaining to yourself in solitary!" she screamed. "We don't tolerate nonsense around here!"

As she marched me off, Daisy Mae finally regained her composure enough to yell after me, "Vicki, you're not going to get away with this. I'll get you!"

Solitary confinement meant a very small room with nothing in it. No bed, no bench, no windows, nothing. Just four walls.

They kept me in solitary for a whole week. I couldn't even go outside for exercise. They would slip my meals through a slot in the bottom of the door. I didn't even see who put them there.

That kind of treatment didn't do much for my anger. I was still mad at the world, mad at the cops, mad at the prison. And now I was especially mad at Daisy Mae. I knew she would be trying to get even with me for what I had done.

I wondered about Daisy Mae. Did she have to serve a week in solitary, too? I was sure going to find out.

When they released me from solitary and I got back to my room, I noticed some extra things there. Evidently I had a roommate now.

A little later, she walked in. I went up to her and stuck out my hand to introduce myself. She jumped back, yelling, "Don't you dare touch me! You're filth, and I don't want anything to do with you!"

"Hey, wait a minute!" I responded. "You've never met me. Who gave you all that information about me?"

"Aren't you Vicki Hensley?" she asked.

"Yeah."

"Well, I've been here for five days now, and I've heard from everybody here that you're bad news," she said. "They all warned me to stay as far away from you as I could."

"Who told you to stay away from me?" I asked.

"Everybody. They said that if I tangled with you, you'd go to the toilets and get the filth out of them and throw it on me. They said you're crazy!"

"Hey, hey, let's wait just a minute," I said. "You and I are going to have to spend a lot of time together in this room, so we might as well start off on the right foot. Let me tell you that story from my point of view. I'm sure it's quite different from what you've been hearing!"

As I related what had happened, I watched her reaction. But I couldn't tell whether or not she believed me.

As I concluded, I said, "Okay, that's my side of the story. Now why don't you tell me your name and let's get acquainted."

"Well, my name is Wigge Anderson. I'm in on a drug charge—possession and sales."

"Me, too," I responded quickly. "At least we have that much in common."

"Is that why you're here?" she asked in surprise. "The girls told me you're here because you're insane—that you flipped your lid and killed somebody."

"Wigge," I said with a laugh, "you know these places. Rumors run rampant. So help me, I am not crazy. I consider myself very normal. There are a few people I might have liked to have killed. But I've never killed anybody. And there's something else I'm not going to do. I'm not going to bow to the system around here. Somebody is messing with my mind about those bathrooms, and that Daisy Mae is going to get it if she doesn't watch out!"

"Hey," Wigge cautioned, "I think you'd better cool it with Daisy Mae. Don't you know she's the one who's really in control around here? Everybody takes orders from Daisy Mae. I've been in prison before, and I can spot who's in charge. Daisy Mae's got this prison wrapped around her little finger. She uses a system of threats and favors to get her way. She can get extra cigarettes. She can get other girls to do her duties. This prison may have a warden, but Daisy Mae is who is really running things!"

So that was it. I had tangled with the top person in the prison system. No wonder I had gotten into trouble!

"Now, Vicki, I don't want to scare you," Wigge went on, "but the word is out that Daisy Mae is going to burn off all of your hair!"

"Burn off all of my hair?"

"Yeah. Because you doused her with filth. After she spent that day in solitary over that incident, she—"

"Wait a minute!" I interrupted. "Wait just a minute! Did I understand you to say that Daisy Mae spent only one day in solitary? I got a week. How come she got only one day?"

Wigge laughed. "As I told you, Vicki, it's the system. I understand she threatened a riot if they didn't let her out. And, let me tell you, she could have done it, too. She's got the power. And the prison authorities know it. So she was let out after a day in solitary!"

It dawned on me that I might have bitten off a bigger chunk than I could chew. I hadn't taken on one person; I had challenged the power of the whole system. Even the authorities were powerless before the threats of someone like Daisy Mae! My life really wasn't worth much, now!

"Do you really think she'd try something like setting my hair on fire?" I asked.

"Vicki, I've been in and out of prisons for the last ten

years. You've got to know something about prison life if
you expect to survive. Of course she will try to set your hair
afire. You see, you've bucked the system. You've threatened her authority. You've made her lose face. So to prove
her authority again, she will have to try something like
this."

My heart beat faster. I had heard about some of the horrible things that went on in prison—about prisoners being
maimed and disfigured and even killed. But here I was—
and it was about to happen to me!

"Setting a person's hair on fire isn't the only thing she
may try," Wigge went on. "Sometimes they'll take a knife
and stab you over and over again. Sometimes there are
gang murders. A whole group of them will pull you into the
shower and beat you until you're dead. Of course, when the
authorities start to ask questions, nobody knows anything.
If anybody squeals, that squealer is marked. They'll kill
her. Vicki, I hate to tell you this, but you've got a serious
problem on your hands."

Now I had really done it. What would it be like to have
my hair burned off? Could I endure pain like that? Likely
I'd be disfigured for the rest of my life. Maybe it would
even kill me.

"Wigge, should I go to the warden?"

"That's the last thing you want to do," she said. "If you
do that, they surely will gang up and kill you."

"Then should I go to Daisy Mae and try to patch things
up?"

"Are you a lesbian?"

"Am I a what?"

"I asked if you're a lesbian."

"Wigge, for crying out loud, I'm no lesbian. Why are you
changing the subject?"

"Well, don't worry; I'm not, either," she told me. "But Daisy Mae is. And she's the worst type—a butch. Now if you go to her to try to patch things up, one of her demands might be that you're going to have to be her girl. Know what I mean?"

I nodded.

"She will capitalize on your coming to her," Wigge went on. "In fact, that may be the reason for this whole confrontation."

Now I really felt sick inside—so sick I wanted to vomit. I couldn't imagine myself in a lesbian relationship with anybody, but most certainly not with fat, ugly, Daisy Mae! Just thinking of her made me nauseated! So no way was I going to go to her to apologize.

That meant I was in a situation with no way out!

I saw Daisy Mae at supper that night—the first time since I had thrown that filth all over her. As I walked by her, she snarled something. I wanted to take my tray and hit her over the head, but I didn't want to go back to solitary.

I had a hard time sleeping that night. I just knew that the moment I closed my eyes, Daisy Mae would suddenly appear and set my hair on fire. Oh, what a horrible thought! My clothes and bedding would probably catch fire, too, and I would burn to death.

So I rolled and tossed and rolled and tossed. But I hadn't had a decent night's sleep in solitary, so I soon found it impossible to keep my eyelids open. I remember thinking, *I'll just close them for a minute, and then. . . .*

Suddenly I smelled smoke. I grabbed for my hair. It was all right. But. . . . Then I spotted it. In the doorway was a lighted candle. But nobody was around.

I jumped out of bed and ran to the hallway. Not a soul.

Everything was peaceful and serene and quiet. But some-body had been here! Daisy Mae! She was trying to scare me into submission!

I grabbed the candle and started to blow it out, but I stopped. I was already in a no-win situation with Daisy Mae. But I wasn't about to be frightened into submission. I'd show her!

Candle in hand, I tiptoed down the hall. None of the rooms had doors on them, and I knew right where Daisy Mae's room was—the biggest and best of them all.

As I got to her room, I heard her snoring. Probably fak-ing. But I spotted her slippers on the floor beside her bed. I walked over, grabbed one, and held the candle flame to it. When it started to burn brightly, I set it in the middle of the room and tiptoed out and back to my bed.

I was going to stand up to Daisy Mae. Whenever she pulled something on me, I was going to do her one better. And I knew she would get the message.

When she spotted me at breakfast the next morning, she blocked my way. I wanted to lower my head and plunge right into her, tray and all. Maybe the hot coffee would spill on her. But I held off.

"You think you're pretty cute, don't you?" she snarled.

"What are you talking about?" I said as innocently as I knew how.

"Don't get smart with me! You know what you did. And you owe me a pair of slippers!"

"Oh, is that what you're talking about?" I answered. "Well, last night I got a little chilly and needed a little fire to keep me warm. I looked around for some firewood, but nobody seemed to have any. The only thing I could find was this dirty, filthy, no-good slipper. I mean, it was so filthy it stunk! I guess the person who wears it must be a real creep. Anyway, I used it to get myself warmed up a little."

"Vicki, that candle was just a warning," she said menacingly. "Either you apologize for what you did to me, or one morning you'll wake up without any of that bleached blonde hair!"

There was no question about it, now. It was exactly as Wigge had said. Daisy Mae wanted me to bow down to her. But if I did, I'd have to be her girl. No way was I going to do that!

"Daisy Mae, you're the lucky one this time," I said quietly. "I should have set your bed on fire and burned you to a crisp!"

"I've got something to tell you, and you'd better listen good, kid," she replied. "You'd better start counting the silverware from breakfast because a knife is going to be missing. I'll get it really sharp, and then I'm going to stab you until your blood runs thick on the floor. You'll be dead before morning because nobody talks to Daisy Mae this way!"

I couldn't back down, now. "You listen to me, Daisy Mae," I growled. "You had better get your girls to count all the matches in this place because tonight I won't stop with just burning one of your slippers. This time it'll be you. You'll burn, baby, burn!"

"You'd better not go to sleep tonight, Vicki," she answered, "because tonight is when I'm going to set your hair on fire. Then we'll see how big and brave you are!"

She wagged her finger at me and sat down. I moved on by and went to another table.

"What was that all about?" Wigge wanted to know.

"Just as you said, Wigge. She wants me to apologize and be her girl. And no way am I going to do that!"

I looked over at Daisy Mae and noticed she was wolfing down everything in sight. I don't know whether the girls at her table wanted their food or not, but she sure was getting anything she wanted from them. But I wasn't about to be her slave.

That night as I got ready to get into bed, I looked over at Wigge and asked, "Do you think I'd look better with short hair?"

"What's the matter, Vicki? Are you scared?"

Of course I was scared, but I sure wasn't going to admit it.

"No, I was just making a joke. I'm not afraid of Daisy Mae."

Wigge was soon asleep, but not me. I was really in a jam. If I fell asleep, Daisy Mae would be in here setting my hair afire. So I rolled and tossed until I was exhausted. The last thing I remember was putting my hand up over my hair.

Suddenly I felt my hand getting hotter. I smelled smoke. There was a flame by my hand! It was really happening!

11

As I felt that hot, burning sensation near my hand, I bolted up in bed. Daisy Mae must have set my hair afire!

But as my head jerked up, a hand slapped across my mouth. By the light of a candle I could make out the face of Daisy Mae. And there was no question about it when she snapped, "One word out of you, Vicki, and it's all over!"

I looked around in terror and noticed that right behind her were two of her biggest, meanest girls. I was no match for three of them. This was it!

Over across the room Wigge had risen on her elbows, staring in disbelief at the scene which was unfolding.

When Daisy Mae realized Wigge was awake, she ordered her to the bathroom. "Stay there until I send word," she said.

Wigge slid out of bed and looked at me helplessly. "Don't hurt her," she pleaded. "She's young and innocent. She doesn't understand the system."

"Don't start ordering me around, Wigge, or you'll be next," Daisy Mae threatened. "I've got a little score to settle here. Nobody's going to throw filth all over me and get by with it!"

When Wigge walked out, Daisy Mae pushed me down on the bed and whispered, "Okay, Vicki, start saying your prayers!" She brought the candle closer to my face, saying, "I'm going to start by burning out your eyeballs. Then I'm going to burn your hair off. Then my friends and I are going to cut your body up into little pieces!"

My eyes grew wide. I knew she was mean enough to do it. Where were those matrons now that I needed them? Probably playing cards. If only I could scream for help.

The flame of the candle was so close that I could feel its heat against my nose. I lunged as hard as I could to get away from it. It caught Daisy Mae by surprise, and her hand slipped off my mouth. I started to scream, but she crammed her hand over my mouth again. Then one of the girls hit me hard right in the stomach. I doubled up in pain.

"One more outburst like that, and I'll drive this knife right through your heart!" Daisy Mae told me. She motioned toward one of her goons who was standing there with the knife and grinning. I knew she would be delighted to get the opportunity to use it!

I strained, hoping to hear the footsteps of a matron making a room check. Had she heard me? Did Wigge go and tell her what was happening? Was she even on my side?

The two goons sat on me to make sure I didn't try anything else. Then Daisy Mae brought the candle up to my face again. I squeezed my eyes shut as tightly as I could. I just knew this fat slob was going to blind me for what I had done to her.

The flame got hotter and hotter. Then I didn't feel it. What was going on?

"Okay, Vicki, you can open your eyes now," Daisy Mae whispered. "I've decided to give you another chance."

That was good news. At least I was going to live a little longer.

"We three are planning to escape," Daisy Mae said in a confidential tone, "and we need you to help us."

I blinked. What was she trying to say? I tried to mumble something, but she still had her hand over my mouth.

"I'm going to take my hand away, Vicki," she said. "If you scream, I'll bloody your pretty little face. I'll break your nose and knock all your teeth out. Then I'll make you eat your teeth. Understand?"

I nodded. I had a lot of spirit, but I also knew it would be ridiculous to try anything in this situation.

She slowly moved her hand away from my mouth. When I didn't scream or try anything, she motioned the two goons to get off me. But Daisy Mae still held the flame close, and the one with the knife kept it poised.

"I said we're escaping, and you're going to help us," Daisy Mae repeated.

"Escape? How in the world are you going to do that?"

"I've got an elaborate plan. You and us are going to break out—"

"Wait a minute," I interrupted. "If you want to break out, that's your business. But I'm not about to try that. I've got too much against me, now. Besides, it'll never work."

"Listen, Vicki," she said, "I know all about you. You've got charges against you a mile long. You're going to rot in jail until you die. You'd better come along with us."

"Daisy Mae, there's no way we can break out of this place. They've got guards and fences and gates. There's no way we can do it!"

"Vicki, I'm giving you a choice. You can come out with us or you can stay here and rot."

"Stay and rot," I answered.

That was the wrong thing, for those two goons jumped onto me again. Daisy Mae pushed the candle toward my face. "Okay, then, rot!" she exclaimed. "But you're going to help us, whether you want to or not!"

I decided that to spare my life I'd better cooperate. "Okay, stay cool," I said. "What am I supposed to do?"

The girls got off my body when I said that. The message was becoming clear. Daisy Mae needed me for something. If I cooperated, I would live a little longer. If I didn't, it was curtains now.

"That's more like it," Daisy Mae said, moving the candle back. "But I want to make one thing perfectly clear. You rat on us, Vicki Hensley, and you're dead! Understand?"

I nodded.

"All right," Daisy Mae went on, "tomorrow you'll be assigned to the yard crew. At exactly four o'clock I want you to be near the middle of the south fence. You know there are two fences there—the inner and outer fences. Well, on the other side of those fences will be two girls on a motorcycle. They are going to throw a gun over the fence. You pick it up and slip it to me later."

"Daisy Mae," I interrupted, "that's crazy. Those guards will be watching our every move—especially with somebody right near the fence. As soon as that gun starts over the fence, those guards will come running. Are you trying to set me up?"

"Not so dumb, Vicki. At the same time, about one hundred yards away, there will be a car with two more of my friends in it. One of them will get out and set off a bunch of big firecrackers. I mean, you'll hear some huge explosions! The guards will come running, all right; but they'll come running toward all the smoke from those firecrackers. That's when the girls will throw the gun over the fence."

That was smart—diverting attention. Maybe it would work.

But suppose it didn't work and the guard saw me pick up the gun? Then I'd be back in solitary and have some more charges to face!

Daisy Mae was waiting for my response. "Suppose I don't cooperate," I said.

She laughed. "You really have no choice—if you want to live!"

"You can't kill me," I said with a lot more bravery than I felt at the moment. "Everybody knows there's bad blood between us. If I'm dead, you're the first one they'll put the screws to."

"I could care less," she answered. "Don't you know why I'm in here, anyway?"

"No, why?"

"I'm in for murder. And so are these two good friends of mine. I figure they're already going to send us up for a long stretch. So what's one more killing? Besides, that's why I'm getting out of here."

"Okay, okay, but what are you going to do with the gun?"

"Very simple. Hostages. As soon as I put that gun up to the brains of these matrons, they'll open the doors and we'll walk out of here. My friends will be waiting outside. It'll be simple."

Could breaking out of jail be that simple? Should I go with them? But if I did, would Daisy Mae settle our score then by killing me? She probably would.

"How can you be so sure it's all going to come off?" I asked. "I've never been on the yard crew."

She laughed and said, "I've got friends in high places, baby." Then she stood up and said, "Don't forget. At four tomorrow you be next to that south fence. Do your part, and I'll let you live. Mess it up, and I'll kill you!" She moved the candle toward me menacingly. Then the three of them walked out.

I broke into a cold sweat realizing what I had just been through and what I was going to have to do as a result of it. I really didn't want to do it, but what choice did I have?

A few minutes later Wigge returned. "What happened?" she asked.

"Oh, just a friendly little conversation."

"Come on, Vicki. I know better. What was that all about?"

"As I said, a friendly conversation."

"I understand," Wigge said, "there's to be an escape tomorrow afternoon. Is that what it was about?"

"Escape?" I asked in surprise as I raised up on my elbows. "Who said there's going to be an escape?"

"Come on, Vicki; it's all over the prison. Everybody's been on a whispering campaign about it all day."

"All over the prison?" I asked in surprise. "Do you suppose the guards know about it?"

"Probably. There's almost always a stool pigeon who will squeal for special favors."

Then it hit me. That Daisy Mae was setting me up! As soon as that gun flew over the fence and I grabbed it, all those guards would be converging on me. I'd have an escape attempt added to my record and be back in solitary. And Daisy Mae would be standing there watching me and laughing as they took me away. That had to be it! This was her way of getting back at me!

I still didn't know if I could trust Wigge. But she had been a real help to me before, so I said, "Okay, I'll level with you. Daisy Mae and her two friends came in here with a big plan to escape. They forced me to agree to help them. But now I see exactly what she had in mind. She's trying to set me up. So I'm not going to go through with it."

"Hey, I'd stay kind of cool on that," Wigge answered.

"Daisy Mae is in here for murder. Same with those other two. They'll do anything to get out of here because they don't have anything to lose!"

"You mean you don't think she's doing it just to set me up?"

"No, I really don't, Vicki. She's got more to gain by getting out of here than by getting back at you. She could find some other way to get you."

"Okay, before I say anything else," I said, "I want to ask you a couple of questions. When you walked out of here and saw me about to be murdered by those three creeps, how come you didn't try to do something to save my life?"

"Vicki, let me tell you something. I told you I've been in and out of prisons for ten years—mostly in. You learn to stay cool in times like this. I knew you weren't going to get killed. It just isn't done that way. Those girls would have gotten you when I wasn't around. Of course, I could have squealed to the matron; but Daisy Mae has so many connections here that it would have turned out to be my word against hers—and I would have come out on the short end."

"What kind of connections does she have?" I asked.

"All kinds. The murderers are at the top of the system; they have the controlling power because they've got nothing to lose. To a certain limit, Daisy Mae will get what she wants."

"Like getting me assigned to the yard crew tomorrow?"

"Listen, she could get you assigned as a secretary in the warden's office; she's got that kind of power. So if she says you are going to be on the yard crew tomorrow, that's where you'll be."

"Well, that's where I'll be," I said. "And this whole thing scares me to death."

"Vicki, you'd better share the plans with me—just in case."

"Just in case what?"

"Just in case there's a big shoot-out and Daisy Mae gets killed. They'll question all the girls, and you may need me to verify what she told you and why you participated."

Could I trust her? Was this her way of weaseling the escape plan out of me? Would she be the one who would rat to the guards?

"Wigge," I said, "I don't know if I can trust you."

"Vicki, you've got to trust me. I'm all you've got. What I really ought to do is just crawl into bed and forget I ever heard anything at all. It's really your problem. But I kind of like you and think you've been getting a raw deal around here. So tell me what is going to happen."

I decided to risk it and told her.

"Sounds pretty chancy to me," she said. "Especially with that gun. There could be a shoot-out, you know."

"I wish you hadn't said that," I responded. "I'm already scared to death about this whole thing."

We both crawled into our beds, but I didn't sleep—and I don't think she did, either.

The following morning, when assignments were given out, I was assigned to the yard crew. All day long we worked around the yard, picking up papers, pulling weeds, raking.

I kept looking at my watch. Four o'clock seemed an eternity away. Finally at about a quarter to four I edged toward the middle of the south fence. Nobody in sight. No motorcycle, no car—nothing. Down at the end of the fence I saw the guard standing on a tower, his rifle at ready.

Five till four—and still nothing. Maybe the whole thing had had to be called off.

At two minutes to four I thought I heard some noise. Sure enough, down the road I spotted a cloud of dust. My heart jammed into my throat. This was it!

Trying hard not to look suspicious, I began to rake like crazy. Out of the corner of my eye I saw a motorcycle come closer and closer, slow, and then stop right opposite me. Two girls got off and stood there hanging on the fence.

Then I noticed a car pull up at the far end and a girl get out of it. Everything was happening just as Daisy Mae had said.

Suddenly there was a deafening explosion—smoke, sparks, and utter confusion. Then a thud. The pistol had landed right next to me.

Sirens screamed. Girls were yelling; guards were shouting. I leaned over to pick up the pistol, but a voice behind me yelled, "Stop or I'll shoot!"

I wheeled around to look into the barrel of a rifle pointed right at me. He didn't have to tell me to throw up my hands.

"One false move, and I'll blast you to smithereens," he said harshly. Then he reached down and picked up the pistol.

With my arms still up I said, "Hey, you won't have any problem from me. I was standing here minding my own business when I heard this deafening explosion and then this thump. I turned around and saw this gun on the ground. I was going to pick it up and take it to the warden."

"Yeah, yeah," he responded. "You can tell the warden all about it. Now move!"

As he marched me toward the warden's office, I noticed that Daisy Mae and her two girl friends were in handcuffs and there were cops all over the place. Evidently somebody had squealed.

I was the last of the yard crew to get to the warden's office. We had to stand in a row facing him. The guards kept their rifles ready.

"All right, girls," the warden said, "there was an attempted escape. It was really stupid. But we are going to find out who was behind this; those people are in real trouble. Now if any of you have been involved, I want you to come and see me this evening. What you tell me will be in strictest confidence. But, so help me, I am going to get to the bottom of this. Those who are responsible will be severely punished. So if you know anything, ask to see me. Remember, it will be in strict confidence."

The warden dismissed us, and we headed back to our cells. Was this all there was to it?

As we were walking down the hall to our rooms, I whispered to one of the girls, "Seems as though we got off easy."

"Baby, it's not over yet!" she whispered back. "The warden works that way—gives you an opportunity to confess. No pressure at first; they wait for the stool pigeons. Anybody involved can get off lighter if they implicate other people; that's the method they use."

I wondered if I should tell the warden what I knew. Would that make it easier when my trial came up? But if I did, would I live long enough for my case to come to trial?

I had visitors again about two the next morning—Daisy Mae and her two friends. "Okay, Vicki, so we got stopped this time," she said, "but that's not going to stop me from getting out of here. So I want you to get something straight. You open your mouth to the warden, and I promise I'll kill you!"

With that, she wheeled around and was gone, taking her two friends with her.

Wigge had taken it all in, so I leaned up on my elbows and asked, "Wigge, if I went to the warden, do you really think she'd kill me?"

"Vicki," she answered solemnly, "I sure do. She'd find a way!"

12

The next few days the whole prison was in an uproar. Rumors ran rampant everywhere—and my name kept cropping up. So any moment I expected to be hauled into the warden's office.

I guess they were biding their time. Maybe they were waiting to see if I would rat on Daisy Mae. Or maybe Daisy Mae had enough power that they were afraid to do anything!

The suspense kept me tossing and turning at night. I suppose part of it was from a guilty conscience—and part from the jam I was in either way. I'd be in trouble with Daisy Mae and the girls if I went to the warden; I'd be in trouble with the authorities if I didn't go to them. I really didn't know what to do.

About a week later, at three in the morning, I couldn't sleep, so I got up and went down to the rest room. I just happened to glance at the shower, and what I saw there made shivers run down my spine. There was a girl in the shower, the shower curtain tied around her neck. She was dangling there, her feet just off the floor.

I ran out of the bathroom to the guard's room, screaming, "Come quickly! Come quickly"

When the matron asked what was wrong, I yelled, "Some girl hanged herself in the shower!"

The commotion brought all the other girls streaming out of their rooms to watch while the matron jerked down the curtain. The girl's body crumpled to the floor, and I got a better look at her. It was Evie Thornton, one of the girls who had come to my room that night with Daisy Mae.

I glanced around at the crowd. Daisy Mae was standing near the back, not showing any emotion at all. That made me wonder. Was this really a suicide? Or was this another of Daisy Mae's warnings to me? If it were that, it sure was a gruesome warning!

Of course, I had to go to the office and file a report. I told exactly what had happened, and the warden seemed to believe me.

At breakfast the major topic was Evie. Some said she had killed herself because she couldn't face life in prison. Some said she was about to admit her part in the escape plan and Daisy Mae had done her in. That made the most sense to me.

To this day I don't know the truth about that situation. But I do know that Daisy Mae wanted me to believe it was a threat because when she passed me in the hallway, she said, "Don't ever forget what happened to Evie. It could happen to you!"

I didn't answer, just walked the other way. I was going to stay as far away from that woman as I possibly could.

That night I still couldn't sleep. Wigge noticed me rolling and tossing. "You need something to help you get to sleep, don't you?" she asked. "Want some Librium?"

"Librium?" I replied in surprise. "How are you going to get them?"

"Did you forget that tomorrow's Sunday?" she replied. "That means we can have visitors. I am having a delivery of Librium made tomorrow. I can get you four, if you want them."

"Say that again."

"My boyfriend, Harry Gilbert, will be coming to see me. When I introduce him to you, I want you to kiss him passionately. He will take it from there."

"You want me to kiss your boyfriend?"

"Yeah. But just one kiss. Now don't ask any more questions."

I never had had any visitors. I assumed Leon was locked up somewhere. I didn't know whether my mother or grandmother even knew where I was—or cared.

But I went to the visiting room with Wigge that Sunday afternoon. Harry was waiting for us. I mostly stood around while he and Wigge talked and kissed. Harry told her he had tried to bail her out, but the bail was too high. I knew what that was about.

When the bell sounded to signal the end of visiting hours, I started looking forward to kissing Harry. He was kind of handsome.

"Harry," Wigge said as we stood to leave, "before you go, my good friend here would like to kiss you. Know what I mean?"

As I stepped toward him, Harry bent over and coughed, putting one hand into his shirt pocket. Then he coughed some more, placing that hand over his mouth. Did the idea of kissing me turn him off that much? Well, when he stopped coughing, he put his arms out. I threw my arms around him, and our lips met. His kiss was so soft and romantic.

Then I felt his tongue touch my lips. I sure didn't know him that well!

I held my teeth tightly together. It felt as though he were trying to push his gum into my mouth. Dumb me! Then it hit me why Wigge wanted me to kiss Harry. This was the way to transfer the Librium!

He pushed one in, then another, until I had all four of them in my mouth. Then he pulled away.

Looking at both of them I said, "You people are brilliant. Thanks for your help."

Harry smiled and said, "Anytime, baby; anytime!"

Then Harry and Wigge kissed again, and we left the room, ready for the matron to search us. I still had the Librium in my mouth.

"Hey, matron, I'll have to introduce you to my boyfriend," Wigge said enthusiastically. "Can that guy kiss! Even Vicki got kissed!"

The matron looked at me and laughed. "I just don't know what I am going to do with you, Wigge," she said. "Your boyfriend keeps turning these girls on. Everybody is going to have to take a cold shower, now!"

Wigge laughed. "Think of the energy we save by not using the hot water!"

Would the matron check my mouth? Well, she ran her hands all over our clothes, but she didn't touch my face. We went on through.

Back in our room I spit out the four pills. "Okay, two for you and two for me," Wigge said.

"How come Harry didn't pass some to you, too?" I asked.

"Vicki, you have a lot to learn about prison life. I set up the deal; you carry it out; we split the profits. Suppose the matron had checked our mouths—you would have gotten busted. But not me."

Well, that certainly was risky for me. But I guess I wouldn't have had anything if Wigge hadn't set up the deal.

"Something else to remember," Wigge went on. "Whenever you get into a tight spot, mention the most obvious thing. You would have thought that the matron would have been tipped off. But it doesn't work that way."

Wigge popped a Librium because she wanted to get high. But I suddenly devised a plan for mine. I would save them. Harry would be back next week, and I could get more.

That night after we were all in bed, the escape bells went off. Was Daisy Mae trying something else? Then on the loudspeaker: "Everybody be calm. We are just testing the system."

"Wigge, what was that all about?" I asked.

"I don't know, but that was no false alarm."

Five minutes later the bells went off again. Then on the loudspeaker: "Everybody to the dining room immediately."

As we headed out our door, Wigge grabbed my arm. "You don't still have those Librium, do you?"

"Yeah, why? They're in the toe of a pair of stockings."

"Better get them out. I have a sneaking suspicion that our rooms are going to be searched. And if they are, there is not one inch the guards won't look through. If they find that Librium, they are going to come down hard on you. So get it out of there, quickly!"

I grabbed the two pills from their hiding place, stuck on a bra, and hid them in it. We then joined the other girls heading for the dining room. At first I couldn't see Daisy Mae anywhere. Then I spotted her off to the back by herself.

When all the girls were in the dining room, the matron shut us in. Then the warden announced, "Okay, ladies, we are having a little shakedown of your rooms. We have reports that drugs are being smuggled in by visitors, so we are now looking for them. If we find any, you will be placed in solitary and the charge will go on your records and be used against you when your cases come to trial."

Some girls glanced around nervously, but I drew a sigh of relief. That Wigge was a smart girl. I was going to keep on listening to her advice.

The warden left, but we were kept in the dining room for two hours. Later he came back with three guards and called out some names. Poor girls. I knew they were going to get it.

When we finally got back to our rooms, Wigge said, "Close, huh?"

"Listen, Wigge, you saved my skin. Maybe I should give you one of these."

"No, that's okay. I can get more."

"But it will be another week until Harry comes back."

"No, not from Harry. I think they're getting onto that, so we'll have to stay cool on it. I've got another connection."

That interested me because I had plans for ten Librium.

"Have you met the dumb nut they have here for a psychiatrist?" Wigge asked. "The guy is a real squirrel. If you go visit him with a big story about some psychological problem, he'll suggest that you take some Librium. I mean, it's so simple, I don't know why everybody hasn't caught on to it. They do keep track of the number of visits, and I'm at my quota. But you could go."

"You mean just go see the psychiatrist and get Librium?"

"Yes, it's that simple. Just make sure you've got a good story."

Good story. Let's see. There was my cancer story that had worked so many times. I suggested it, but Wigge said I looked too healthy. Besides, all the psychiatrist would do would be to suggest a physical examination. It had to be something psychological.

"Wigge," I said, "I've been thinking that the only way for me to get out of this place is to wrap a shower curtain around my neck—"

"For crying out loud, don't try it!" she interrupted. "With your luck, all you'd get would be a sore neck."

"No, no, I don't really mean I'll do it," I said. "I was just thinking up something to tell the psychiatrist. After all, I was the one who found Evie, and it has been preying on my mind. . . ."

"Great!" Wigge responded. "Suicide always drives psychiatrists bananas. And you can bet that it makes the warden nervous, too. I know that Evie's suicide made all the papers. Another one would probably bring an investigation. So the warden probably has passed on instructions to keep anyone thinking of suicide doped up! I think you've got it, kid."

After breakfast I asked a matron if I could talk to the psychiatrist. When she asked why, I said, "Ever since I found Evie, I keep getting more and more depressed. I can't sleep. And I get this overwhelming urge to kill myself."

She told me to wait in her office while she checked. About ten minutes later she returned with a small man. A fringe of long, graying hair encircled his shiny head. Glasses hung askew on his nose, and he kept pushing them back into place.

"I'm Dr. Stillwell," he announced. "You wanted to talk with me?"

I assumed he was the psychiatrist, so I nodded. He told me to follow him to his office, which was in another building.

When we finally came to it, he opened the door and motioned me inside. Sure enough, there was the couch—just as I expected. He pointed to it, and I sat on the edge. He walked over, patted my arm, and said, "Now, Vicki, the first thing I want you to do is relax. Don't be nervous. Just lie down on the couch."

I obeyed, but I wasn't very relaxed. Just being around this doctor made me nervous. He might find my pose rather inviting.

He eased himself onto a chair next to me, pulled a pad and pen from his desk, and said, "Vicki, tell me what's troubling you."

"Well," I said, "ever since I've been in this place the pressure has been building up on me. I know I've done wrong and I deserve to be here. But I can't sleep. I can't take the pressure." I looked over at him. "You know about that girl Evie who hanged herself in the shower?"

"Oh, yes," he answered. "Most unfortunate. I'm sure I could have helped her if she had come to me."

"Well, I was the one who found her," I said. "I went down to the rest room because I couldn't sleep, and I found her hanging there. Now something keeps forcing me down there in the middle of the night. I stand there looking at that spot, and I'm starting to see myself hanging there like that. I just know that one of these days I won't be able to resist the pressure!"

I noticed the deep lines etched in his face as he wrote furiously. It looked as though my story was working.

"Why would you want to kill yourself?" he asked gently.

"As I told you, I can't stand the pressure. There's something within me that's telling me it's the only way out. I can't sleep."

He asked me some more questions, and I couldn't tell for

sure how he was reacting. Maybe if I tried something different. I sat up on the couch, looked as wild-eyed as I could, and said, "Dr. Stillwell, I'm going to kill you. I can't stand anyone prying into my private life this way. Then I'm going to kill myself."

I got off the couch and edged toward him. He got up and started backing away toward his desk.

"Now, see here," he said. "You take one more step toward me, and I'll push this button. Then some big, burly guards will come in and take you to solitary. So you'd better settle down right now. Get back on that couch!"

I stared at his finger poised on the button. I sure didn't want solitary again. So I bent over and started to sob—and I really knew how to make the tears come.

He placed his hand on my shoulders and said, "Now, now, Vicki, everything is going to be all right." Then he gently led me back to the couch and got me to lie down.

But I kept sobbing. "I don't know what comes over me, doctor," I said. "I just can't help myself."

He asked me about my childhood, about my mother and my relationship with her. He had a field day with that. Then he said, "I want you to come back and talk to me at two tomorrow. I think if we have some sessions together, they'll help us work this thing out. And, Vicki, you've got to learn to trust me."

"Okay," I agreed. "But I know I won't be able to sleep again tonight. Could you prescribe a little something for me to get me over the hump?"

"Sure," he replied. "I was getting to that."

"You think a couple of Librium will be okay?" I asked.

"No problem."

He fumbled through his keys, went over and unlocked a little chest, pulled out a large bottle, and handed two Librium to me. "Take these before you go to bed," he said. "They'll put you to sleep."

I didn't take the Librium. Instead I stashed them away with the two I already had. Only six to go now.

The following day I had another session with Dr. Stillwell and asked him for more Librium. He seemed to understand—especially when I told him I was sleeping so much better now. By the end of my fourth session that week, I had my ten Librium. That evening I would carry out my plan. Finally I would have peace.

After supper I walked to the rest room and went inside one of the shower stalls. After I closed the curtain, I popped all ten of those pills. That was my plan. The ten Librium would do me in. Dr. Stillwell would be an accomplice to my suicide!

I ambled out of the rest room down to the TV room where six of the girls were watching some stupid quiz show. I sat on the floor a few feet from the set and started to get high. Then giddy.

The rush hit me quickly. I hadn't had any drugs in my body for a while, so I knew it would be that way. I felt myself losing consciousness. Those green and black capsules had done their job.

When I opened my eyes, I became aware of a lot of confusion. A couple of girls and a matron were leaning over me, and I heard a voice that seemed to come out of a hollow barrel saying, "I think she's coming out of it."

I blinked my eyes to try to clear the blur. Hey, I was in my own bed in my own room. The matron kept asking, "Vicki, Vicki; are you all right, now?"

Anger flashed through me. I had wanted to die. It looked like the only way out for me. But I had failed at that, too.

The matron grabbed my arm and pulled me off the bed.

"The warden wants to see you right now!" she announced coldly.

My knees were so shaky I could hardly walk. That didn't matter to her. She was infuriated that I had tried suicide, and she was taking her anger out on me. She led me at breakneck speed to the warden's office.

Still holding me by the arm, she knocked on his door. When he said, "Come in," she opened the door and pushed me in. "This is the girl," she told him.

He pointed to a chair and commanded, "Sit down." I was only too glad to obey. I don't think I could have stood. He sat on the corner of his desk and said, "Caledonia, tell me what happened."

"She tried to commit suicide. She passed out in the TV room. We got the doctor and pumped out her stomach. Apparently she had taken ten Librium."

The warden looked at me and snarled, "Is that right?"

I stared at the floor. They had the evidence if they had pumped my stomach. What could I say?

When I didn't respond, the warden jumped down from his perch, moved right next to me, grabbed me by the hair, and jerked my head up to where I had to look at him. "Young lady, when I talk to you, I expect you to look at me, and I expect an answer," he shouted. "Now answer me!"

When I looked into his face, it was contorted with rage, but I didn't respond. So he began to twist my hair. Oh, it hurt! So I finally answered softly, "Yes, sir, I did try to kill myself."

With that admission he exploded. "Listen, I ought to slap you up against that wall for trying something so stupid!" he shouted. "Don't you know we've already had enough publicity about suicides in this place for me to lose my job? Already there's a big investigation going on. All I need right now is another suicide."

"I'm sorry, sir," I said softly. "I really wasn't thinking about your problems."

Ignoring my comment, he continued to rant and rave. "I'm going to throw you into solitary and keep an eye on you," he shouted. "There's no way you can commit suicide there! We're not going to have this nonsense going on around here. I'll make an example of you!"

He let go of me, and I stared back at the floor again. "What do you think we ought to do with you?" he snarled.

I didn't know it was a rhetorical question, so I blurted out, "Let me go, I guess."

That was too much for him. He grabbed my chin and jerked it up toward him. Getting his face practically into mine he shouted, "It's about time you got your life together!"

I looked at him sullenly. No way was my life ever going to get together. All I had to look forward to was rotting in jail. I had failed this time, but I wouldn't let up until I did find a way to kill myself.

"Get her out of here," the warden ordered. "Put her in solitary for two weeks."

Caledonia grabbed me roughly and pushed me down one hall after another until we got to solitary. There she opened the door and shoved me inside. Once again I had nothing but four bare walls.

The sound of the door slamming behind me made me realize again that nobody really cared what happened to me. The only reason the warden was upset over my attempted suicide was that it made him look bad. My suicide could have been the thing that got him fired. He sure didn't care about me.

Two weeks in solitary were hell on earth. I knew a little about it from that week I had spent there earlier. The only contact with humanity was seeing a tray of food slipped through a little opening in the door. I figured there had to be a person out there pushing the food in, but I never saw or heard anyone.

So that tray of food sliding in was the only bright spot in a day. And sometimes they'd forget to bring it. What could you do about it? Nothing. Who could you complain to?

It was awful there. No showering, no washing, no exercise. But most of all the loneliness and boredom got to me. Nothing to do. No one to talk to. I could easily go crazy if I were there long.

I spent the lonely, boring hours figuring out another way to commit suicide. But nothing seemed to be the right way. Besides, they'd really be watching me, now.

Those two weeks seemed like twenty years. But finally the day came when someone unlocked the door and the first human voice I had heard in two weeks—other than my own—said, "Okay, you can go back to your room."

As I left that cell, I told myself they would never get me back in there again. I would kill myself—even if it was with something as chancy as that shower curtain.

13

As I walked back into my room, Wigge greeted me with, "Vicki, it's good to have you back. I thought they were going to put you away forever. I guess you're lucky it was only two weeks."

"Yeah," I answered lamely. "It seemed like twenty years."

I couldn't return her enthusiasm because I was still mad and hurt. I simply stalked to the edge of my bed and sat there sullenly.

Then I noticed an open book on her bed. Strange. Never before had I seen her interested in reading anything.

"What's with the book?" I asked.

She picked it up lovingly and said, "That's my Bible."

"Bible?" I asked in surprise, and then fell laughing onto my bed. "Wigge, you've really freaked out, haven't you? This place has finally gotten to you, too. That's the funniest thing I've heard in the last two weeks!"

She didn't respond—just smiled. I stared at her. There was something so different about her smile. Her eyes mirrored peace—something I had never seen there before.

"What kind of pills are you on?" I asked.

"Pills? I'm not on any kind of pills," she replied sweetly. "I don't need them anymore, Vicki. Something happened to me while you were gone."

"Yeah, I can tell you're different, somehow. What happened?"

"Vicki, I got saved!"

"Saved? Saved from what?"

"Vicki, I've been born again. I've taken Jesus as my Saviour, and He's taken away all my sins!"

"What?" I yelled, almost in shock. "You got jailhouse religion?"

Smiling again she said, "Call it what you wish, Vicki. But whatever it is, I have a peace in my heart that I have never had before. I know Jesus put it there."

"Oh, come on, Wigge," I argued. "I've seen girls get jailhouse religion before. It usually lasts for two or three days. But when the pressure of these bars keeps them locked in, that religion doesn't do them any good. I think they're all hypocrites. They're just using religion to try to get on the good side of the judge. You've been around longer than I have. You know that's the truth."

"I know that what I've got is something I've never had before," she replied. "And I know it's just what you need to melt that anger and frustration out of you."

That did it! I jumped up and stomped out of the cell. Even solitary confinement would be better than being cooped up with a Jesus freak! I knew she would keep on preaching at me, and I sure couldn't take that!

I had to get rid of her. No way was a religious nut going to share my cell!

I needed time to formulate a plan. Hey, I could shower and do some thinking at the same time. After all, it had been two weeks since I had been allowed to shower, and I sure didn't smell very good—not even to me.

When I walked back into our room, Wigge didn't even look up. Nor did she preach at me. So I just grabbed some clean clothes and my bathrobe and headed for the shower.

Someone else was in there. I remember fleetingly thinking that was rather strange. Most of the girls didn't shower at this time of day. But there were no rules against it.

I undressed, went into a shower stall, and turned on the water. Oh, it felt good. I lathered and lathered and lathered my hair and my body. I didn't know if I ever wanted to get out.

The water was splashing across my face when someone parted the shower curtain. A voice too deep to be a girl's voice said, "Hi, baby; what's up?"

I opened my eyes and looked into the face of a girl with short hair. But suddenly I realized she was completely naked standing there, and nobody needed to give me a lesson in anatomy! I was staring at a naked man!

I screamed, leaped out of the shower, grabbed my robe, and put it on as I ran down the hall. How did a man ever get into the shower in a women's prison?

I started for the guard's room to tell a matron. But I decided not to. The whole idea was totally preposterous. What if there was nobody there when I took the matron back in? She would say I was hallucinating and might try suicide again. Maybe it was a trap to get me back into solitary.

Congratulating myself on my cleverness in seeing through this plot by the prison officials, I headed instead back to my room. I knew Wigge would still be there. I'd get her to corroborate my story before I rushed off to the matron.

"Wigge," I said breathlessly as I ran into our room, "you won't believe this, but there's a man taking a shower down there in the women's rest room."

"You're kidding!"

"Come on," I said. "I'll show you."

She jumped up and started out the door.

"Careful," I cautioned, grabbing her by the arm. "I think he might have rape on his mind."

We moved carefully down the hall toward the rest room. As we neared the door, I saw him coming out.

"That's him, Wigge!" I whispered—relieved that she could see him, too. "Let's get the matron."

I started to run, but she grabbed my arm. "Hold it, Vicki. Everything's okay."

The guy came toward us and said nonchalantly, "Oh, hi Wigge. Who's the chick?"

I wanted to spit in his face. No way was this guy going to call me a chick. I knew what he had on his mind when he pulled that shower curtain back on me! I backed up against the wall. So help me, if he tried anything, I was going to kick him good.

"Wigge, who's the chick?" he demanded again. "Does she belong to you?"

Wigge laughed. How dare she laugh about a serious matter like this?

"Vicki," she said, "this is a new inmate here, Jean Hockett."

He held out his hand, but I kept mine stiff at my side. No way was I going to touch this creep.

"Vicki, don't you want to get acquainted with Jean?" she asked. I shook my head stiffly and edged away.

"Don't worry, Jean," Wigge said. "She'll get over it."

With that, Jean walked on down the hall and into a room. I stood there staring after her.

"For crying out loud, Wigge," I said after he had disappeared, "what are they doing putting a man in a women's prison?"

"Calm down," Wigge said. "Jean isn't a man."

"Oh, come on, now," I replied. "I saw him naked in there in that shower. I know a man when I see one." I felt like running down to Jean's room, ripping off his bathrobe, and saying, "See, Wigge, see? Jean is a man!"

She must have known what I was thinking because she said, "This may take a little getting used to, but Jean is a transsexual."

"A what?"

"A transsexual. In Jean's case it's a guy who felt more like a girl and had an operation to turn him into a girl. You know what I mean?"

Well, it was a little confusing, but I had heard of such things before. But I had never encountered one in the shower before, and what I saw didn't look much like a girl!

"I know what you're going to say, Vicki," she went on. "I saw the same thing. It was a lousy operation."

"This is the craziest thing I ever heard of," I yelled. A creep like that should be done away with!"

"Now take it easy, Vicki," she said softly. "Jesus died for Jean as well as for you."

"I just can't understand you and this Jesus stuff!" I exploded. "How could anyone love a creep like Jean? I wish you could have been there when he or she or whatever it is opened the shower curtain and stared at my body! He had other things on his mind! And you are trying to tell me Jesus died for him? That guy ought to be electrocuted!"

"My goodness," Wigge responded, "Jesus not only needs to save you but He also needs to give you some compassion, Vicki. I just wish you could have been in our room a couple of nights ago when Jean came in and told me some of the horrible things she's been through."

"What are you talking about? I don't have time to talk to

transsexuals. They all ought to be—"

"Vicki, don't talk that way," she interrupted. "Let me tell you about Jean."

I admit that my curiosity was aroused. I really didn't know anything about transsexuals. And I figured I was going to have to be around one whether I liked it or not. So I said, "Okay, but let me go back to the shower and get the rest of the shampoo out of my hair. My shower was somewhat interrupted."

When I got back to our room, I perched myself on my bed and started combing out my hair. "I'm ready for your story, now," I said.

"Well," Wigge began, "when Jean was a small boy, he loved to play with dolls. When he became a teenager, he said he felt more like a girl than a boy. Whenever he put on women's clothes, he felt comfortable. When he put on men's clothes, he felt uncomfortable. So he decided that he was really a girl, not a boy."

"Oh, come on, Wigge. All of us struggle with identity."

"Maybe so, but Jean went to his dad, who was a college professor. I just can't believe what he told Jean. He said that whatever he felt like, that's what he should do."

"What did he mean by that?"

"Well, he was saying that if Jean felt like a girl, he should be a girl; if Jean felt like a boy, he should be a boy. So Jean decided to be a girl, adopted a girl's name, and always dressed like a girl. She was already out of high school, but it wasn't working out around home and her old friends, so she ran away. Of course, she had some terrible emotional problems and got into drugs. That was the only way she could get relief.

"Well, she eventually got busted, and the authorities treated her like a man and threw her into a men's prison.

By this time she had been living as a girl for several years. Well, you wouldn't believe what she had to go through in that men's prison. It was indescribable!"

I could imagine the problems.

"Well, when Jean got out," Wigge continued, "she decided she had to have an operation that would change her into a girl. But she didn't have much money, and the people who worked on her really mutilated her—as you noticed. But she got medical papers to prove she really was a girl. Well, she was still into drugs, and she got busted again a few days ago. This time, because she had papers proving she was a woman, they put her in here. But it obviously hasn't solved her problem."

"You can say that again," I offered. "I wish you could have been in that shower when I first saw her. When she opened that shower curtain, I could tell what was on her mind, or his mind, or whoever's mind in an instant. What I read in those eyes was that here was a person with a dirty, filthy mind."

"I think you're jumping to conclusions, Vicki," Wigge countered. "You were startled—shocked—by what you saw. I think if you knew Jean as I do, you would realize she was only trying to be friendly. She has faced so much rejection in her life that it makes her act a little strange and a little abrupt. But she's a real person, Vicki, and she's got tremendous hurts."

I put my comb down and nodded. "Maybe I was a little hasty," I admitted. "I know I sure was shocked by what I saw."

"Vicki," Wigge went on, "you were probably so busy looking elsewhere that you didn't notice the bad scars on Jean's wrists."

I certainly hadn't.

"Next time take a look at her arms, if you can. You'll see they really are scarred. She told me she's tried to commit suicide at least ten different times. Another thing—look at the right side of her face. There's a deep scar there, too. Once she put a gun to her head and pulled the trigger. Something startled her as she did it, and the bullet just grazed her skull. And if I read her right, Vicki, I think she's still out to kill herself."

She seemed to look through me. I wondered if she knew I was still plotting suicide, too. It seemed like the only way out. I could sure sympathize with Jean on that.

"When she told me all this," Wigge went on, "I had the opportunity to share with her how Jesus could forgive her sins and help her solve all her problems. She broke down and cried like a baby. I guess she never before felt that anyone cared about her. Can you imagine the horrible time she must be having trying to figure out who and what she really is? I can't begin to understand."

"Neither can I," I chimed in.

"But Jesus understands," Wigge said with confidence. "And Jean and I have agreed that we are going to pray about her problem—that even though she's in this terrible, mixed-up emotional state, she will receive God's grace to sustain her. You know, Vicki, I believe now that no problem is too great for the Lord. I mean, *no* problem!"

The way she looked at me, I got her drift. But I wondered. Could Jesus possibly solve my problem?

I didn't have to ask her. I knew the answer. My problem was too big for anybody to solve. And I didn't think her Jesus could do anything about the mess Jean was in, either.

"Vicki, wouldn't you like to receive Jesus as your Saviour and find real peace?" Wigge pressed. "You know, I've already found that if you receive Jesus, you may be in prison, but the prison isn't in you. And that makes all the difference in the world."

Where had I heard that before? Somewhere—but I couldn't place it.

"Jesus will give you peace—the kind of peace that will make you contented no matter what," Wigge continued.

I jumped off the bed and shouted, "Get off my case, Wigge. I really don't believe all that about your Jesus, so quit preaching!"

"Okay, okay," she responded. "But you can't keep me from praying for you. I know Jesus has a better life for you."

I stomped off to the TV room, but I couldn't get my mind off what she had said. Could Jesus really help me?

Something happened the next day that blew my mind. Jean got religion, too. Or, as Wigge expressed it, she "accepted Jesus as Saviour." Suddenly that girl with all those huge problems seemed so happy and relaxed. I couldn't believe it.

True to her word, Wigge didn't preach at me. But she and Jean often got together in our cell for a Bible study. I'd pretend to be busy reading or doing something else, but I was fascinated by some of the things they were talking about.

They both had a great peace about life, now. Their reactions to the frustrations of prison life were so different from what they had been. Was it really true that Jesus could do this for a person? Or was it a kind of self-hypnosis?

They said it was Jesus. And I had to admit—to myself, at least—that I was seeing some pretty strong evidence of that truth. But would it work for me?

Some people from a New Orleans church had started a Sunday-afternoon service in the chapel, and Wigge and Jean attended faithfully. They would invite me, but I always had an excuse.

Well, one Sunday afternoon I was lying on my bunk staring at the ceiling, bored out of my gourd. So when Wigge grabbed her Bible and headed out the door and said, "Hey, why don't you join us in the chapel this afternoon?" I surprised myself by saying yes. Another thing—I had gotten word that my court date was coming up in two weeks and I was getting nervous about that, too. Would it settle my fate—a lifetime in prison?

As I swung my legs over the side of the bed, Wigge said, "Well, praise the Lord. He is answering our prayer."

"What did you say?" I asked.

She just smiled. I found out later that the two of them had been praying that I would agree to go with them that day.

"You picked a great day to come, Vicki," Wigge told me. "We're going to have a special guest—a Mom Benton from the Walter Hoving Home."

I never got very excited about mothers because of the relationship I had had with my own. So I wondered aloud why this mom was special.

"Oh, Mom Benton and her husband have a large home for girls in Garrison, New York," Wigge told me. "Here, take a look at this."

From her dresser she picked up a book. I noticed a very attractive girl on the cover. "Mom Benton's husband writes about girls like us," she said. "This one's about Lori. She really went through some problems in life."

She handed me the book, and I studied the cover. It

looked like any other paperback on the newsstands. Only this Lori looked a lot like me. I started to thumb through the book, and one of her experiences caught my eye, and I started reading.

"Not now," Wigge said, pulling the book from my hands. "When you start one of John Benton's books, it's hard to put it down until you're finished. There'll be plenty of time for you to read this, later. Right now it's more important that you come to chapel!"

Wigge grabbed my arm and headed me out the door and down the hall. "They call this woman Mom B and her husband Brother B," she explained. "They were down speaking at a church in New Orleans this weekend, and the people were able to arrange for them to come out for our chapel. This is a treat of a lifetime. I'm really looking forward to meeting them."

"You mean the guy who wrote the book is going to be here, too?"

"Right. They both are."

Wow! I was going to meet an author! I'd never met one before, and I found myself really getting excited.

A lot more girls than usual seemed to be heading for chapel. I guess the word had gotten around. I heard later that a number of the girls had already read some of Reverend Benton's books. The church people had been bringing books out with them for several weeks now, and the girls had been passing them around.

Jean joined us as we walked along—all smiles. I just couldn't get over the change that Jesus had made in her life.

When we got to the chapel, Wigge introduced me to Sheila Sandburg, the woman from the church who was responsible for the services. She had such a graciousness and compassion about her that I loved her from the moment I met her.

Sheila introduced us to the Bentons. I extended my hand to Mom Benton, but before I knew what was happening, she had her arms around me, saying, "Vicki, you are so precious. I just know the Lord has a wonderful plan for your life."

She seemed so alive, so joyful. So did her husband. They were both younger than I had imagined. I guess when Wigge had said "Mom," I visualized some grandmotherly type. But these two people sure were able to relate to us.

In fact, Mom Benton didn't seem to care whom she hugged. I watched when Sheila introduced Jean to them. Reverend Benton shook hands, but Mom Benton hugged Jean. I thought, *If she only knew she was hugging a man!* I guess Reverend Benton didn't have any idea he was watching his wife hug another man. Well, I sure wasn't going to tell him.

By then it was time for the service to start. Sheila led us in singing what they called choruses. We didn't have the hymnbooks they had had at the few church services I had ever been to. Everybody knew the words, I guess. And they sure sang with enthusiasm. Some of them even clapped their hands in rhythm. I didn't know anybody enjoyed religion. I had always thought it was something people tolerated.

When Mom Benton was introduced, she told how she became a mother to hundreds of delinquent girls. It was so interesting to hear her tell of her experiences. "There are two things I've found that all girls really need," she said. "They need Jesus, and they need love."

I knew I needed love, but I wasn't sure about Jesus. But

Mom B told how it was Jesus who had changed the girls and had given them hope and a purpose in life.

Then Reverend Benton spoke. He didn't preach at us the way I expected. Mostly he told us about a girl named Winnie Gerdon who had gone through the program at the Walter Hoving Home.

The name rang a bell. And as he related her story, I remembered those three detectives telling me about her and about the Walter Hoving Home. Strange that I should be hearing all this again and under such different circumstances.

I hadn't ever thought back to that conversation with those three detectives until this very moment. Now every detail about Winnie came back to me just before the Reverend Benton told about her.

He told about the visit he and Mom Benton made after she was put into the federal penitentiary—how when she came to see them, she was smiling and telling them how she felt this was God's will for her life.

"Friends, I will never forget what she told me," he said. "She said, 'Brother B, I may be in prison, but the prison isn't in me!' Hallelujah! Jesus sets us free no matter where we are!"

There it was again: *You may be in prison, but with Jesus, the prison isn't in you!*

Then he told how the prison officials themselves worked to get Winnie released because of her above-reproach conduct and her radiant attitude. "But," he said, "I am convinced that if Winnie had had to stay in prison, she would still have felt the same way. She looked upon prison as her mission field. She had a tremendous influence while she was there."

I glanced over at Wigge. Little tears were rolling down

her cheeks, and she was smiling. So was Jean. Somehow they could really relate to what he was saying.

Then he asked those girls who wanted to receive Jesus as their Saviour to raise their hands. We were supposed to have our heads bowed and eyes closed, but I sneaked a look around and noticed that several girls raised their hands. I felt something tugging inside of me, telling me that was what I should do. But something else told me it would never work for me. This may sound crazy, but I began to argue with myself. If this could help Wigge and Jean, I reasoned, why couldn't it help me? I guess at the time I must have thought that it was just too good to be true.

The girls who raised their hands were invited to go forward for prayer. Reverend and Mrs. Benton and Sheila prayed with them. Even Wigge and Jean went up there to pray with the girls. I didn't understand what was going on, but those girls sure seemed to get excited about it all.

I just sat in my seat, staring at the tile floor. I was a little confused over what I had seen and heard that afternoon. And uppermost in my mind wasn't Jesus. It was the date I had coming up in court in two weeks. I knew I would be going to prison for many, many years. There was no way I could get out of it. My court-appointed attorney hadn't even mentioned plea bargaining. I had blown that chance.

I was so intent on my thoughts that I didn't realize someone had sat down next to me. She asked, "Can I talk to you for a minute?" I looked into the smiling eyes of Mom Benton.

I wanted to shout, "No, you can't!" I wanted to run out of the chapel and back to the security of my cell. I knew there was no way I could be helped. Reverend Benton could get teary eyed over somebody strong like Winnie, but

I wasn't that type. If I got a long prison term, I would be in prison and the prison would be in me!

When she saw I was trying to ignore her question, Mom B put her arm around my shoulder and hugged me. "Vicki," she said, "all during this service God has been talking to me about you. He told me you have a deep need in your life, that you're worried about the future. He told me to tell you that Jesus really loves you; that no matter what the future holds, He wants to go with you. I really don't know much about you, Vicki, but I know Jesus wants to be your Friend. He can bring you peace that you've never known."

It all sounded so simple, so pat. Just let Jesus come in. He will give you peace. But I didn't believe it could happen to me.

"Vicki, can I introduce you to a Friend of mine?" Mom B asked.

I looked around. Friend? There was nobody standing there!

14

When Mom B saw me looking around, she smiled and said, "The Friend I want to introduce you to is Jesus."

"I don't need Him," I said. "Jesus is only for those who are scared and afraid."

She smiled again. "I guess you might say He is for that kind of people," she admitted. "But they are not the only ones! There are so many benefits to anyone who comes to Jesus because He can give you peace, no matter what your problems are."

I figured if I sounded tough I would get rid of her. As soon as I got back to my cell, I was shutting these religious nuts out of my life forever. So I clammed up and put on my toughest face.

She still had her arm around my shoulders, and she gave me another little squeeze. "You know, Vicki, it's normal to sound tough and hard—as though we're capable of handling our own lives. But down deep inside I can sense that you're hurting—and hurting badly. You're scared. But Jesus wants to take all that fear and turn it into love. He wants to exchange all your sin and evil for His righteousness. He wants to come into your life and give you hope."

This woman was something else. It was almost as if my life were an open book to her. Well, I was still going to put up a tough front.

"Hey, listen, man," I said in my toughest voice, "I'm all right. In a few more days I'll be out of this jail and on my own. I have lots of plans. Life will be great."

She just smiled and said, "I hope that happens, Vicki. But supposing it doesn't, and the judge sends you away for a long, long time? What, then?"

She had me there. I tried to mumble an answer, but nothing came out. I had to find something. Then I thought of it—it was the perfect way to get her off my case. She would be so horrified that she'd take off.

"Did you know that before the service you were hugging a man?"

"You mean here in this chapel?"

"Yes!" I had her now!

"Who? What?"

"You know that Jean Hockett? She's really a man."

I watched to see how she would react. This was going to be interesting.

Well, would you believe she just sat there, smiling at me? Didn't this woman ever lose her cool and quit smiling?

"Oh, yes, Jean Hockett," she said matter-of-factly. "Sheila told us about her on the way over here today. I understand that Jean had asked the authorities for someone to counsel with her, and this past week they let Sheila have some time with her. That story about Jean is one of the saddest I've ever heard. But the beautiful part is that Jean now has Christ. He is able to heal all those scars in her life. She has that peace now—that peace I've been telling you about, Vicki. I know you don't begin to have the same kind of problems Jean has—not a beautiful girl like you. But you need Jesus every bit as much as Jean does."

I wasn't going to let her get by that easy. "Didn't you feel clammy or dirty, hugging her?" I asked.

"Of course not," Mom B responded. "I just wish you could understand and experience the kind of love Jesus

puts within us. It's not like anything you've ever known.
You see, when Jesus comes into our hearts, He helps us to
love everybody. And I mean *everybody*. It's not really us so
much who's loving these people; it's His love in us. His love
reaches everybody in this world. It doesn't matter if the
person is a transsexual, a lesbian, a murderer, an alcoholic,
a drug addict, whatever. Even if you could think of something worse than all those put together, Jesus still loves that
person. In fact, He loves you so much, Vicki, that He died
on the cross for your sins. He loves you just the way He
loves Jean. Oh, if you could only experience His love, it
would be so much better than for me to try to explain it to
you."

She threw both arms around me again and drew me
close. "Vicki," she said in a way that made me believe her,
"Jesus loves you, and I love you, too."

I couldn't understand why someone cared that much
about me. But as she hugged me close, a dam broke inside
me. Tears gushed from my eyes as I began to weep uncon-
trollably.

She squeezed me again. It felt so good. Then she patted
me on the back, telling me, "Vicki, I love you the same as I
love my own children. And I wish I could help you to understand this, but Jesus' love for you is even greater than
my love for you."

I don't know how long she held me in her arms. It felt
so good, so comforting and reassuring. Then I finally regained my composure and leaned back against the bench.

"Wouldn't you like to receive Jesus as your Saviour right
now?"

I wanted to say yes, but something inside wouldn't let
me. "Mom B," I explained, "if I did that now, somebody
would say I was just using Jesus as an escape. I have no

time for jailhouse religion!"

"Oh, that's a normal response, Vicki," she replied, seemingly unimpressed by my argument. "And it's true that some people do use Jesus as an escape hatch. Maybe you've heard of soldiers in wartime who had what was called 'foxhole religion.' While the bullets were whizzing over their heads and the bombs and shells were exploding near their foxholes, they made all sorts of promises to God about what they would do if He got them out of this jam. But as soon as the war was over and the danger was past, they forgot all about God and their promises to Him. The Lord knows that."

"But then why should I receive Jesus now? Shouldn't I wait until after my court case and then do it?"

Oh, oh! Too late I realized I had just admitted that I wasn't about to get out of prison, as I had told her. And she didn't seem at all surprised.

"That's something people don't seem to understand about Jesus," she told me. "Jesus didn't say He'd come to save us in prison and get us out. He came to save us so that we might be able to endure anything we have to go through. There are people in prison who will probably be in prison for the rest of their natural lives. They know that. But if they're Christians, Jesus is there with them. Remember what my husband said a little while ago? You may be in prison, but the prison doesn't have to be in you! That is true; it's happening in the lives of many people even while I'm here talking to you. The people who have experienced this know the peace that Jesus gives. He gives them grace, which helps them withstand all the problems of the prison system. These people are model prisoners, yet they probably won't get out. They're like Winnie—you know, the girl Brother B talked about today. While she was in prison, she became a tremendous witness for Christ and had an influence on many, many people. Vicki, that's what Jesus wants to do for you. Whether you spend the rest of your life in prison, or whether you get out tomorrow, no matter what happens, Jesus Christ will give you the grace and strength to become the person He wants you to be. Believe me, it is possible to live a meaningful life that is pleasing to Him and to the people around you—even in prison."

I was hanging onto every word, hoping against hope it was true. It seemed as though it made sense. But would it work?

"Vicki," Mom B said, seeming to sense my doubts, "why don't you just give Christ a chance? If it doesn't work, it doesn't work. But what have you got to lose? Just give Him a chance."

That made sense. What did I have to lose? So I said, "Okay, I'll try it. What do I do?"

"It's a lot easier than you think," she replied. "Let me explain."

She reached into her purse and pulled out a small Bible and flipped it open. "There's a verse here in the Bible— Romans 3:23—that says, 'For all have sinned, and come short of the glory of God.' Something deep within us tells us we are sinners. Don't you agree?"

"No problem there," I responded. "I know I've sinned."

She flipped to something near the back of the Bible. "Then here in 1 John 1:9 is something that gives us sinners hope," she told me. "It says, 'If we confess our sins, he [God] is faithful and just to forgive us our sins, and to cleanse us from all unrighteousness.' Now, Vicki, from the Scriptures I have given you the first two steps."

"Two steps?" I asked in surprise.

"Yes, two. Let's go over them again. The first thing you

have to do is to admit you're a sinner."

"Okay, I have that."

"The second thing you have to do is to confess your sins to Jesus, believing that when you do that, He will forgive them."

I looked a little puzzled, so she read 1 John 1:9 again. This time I could see what she was driving at—that if I confessed my sins to Jesus, He had promised He would forgive them and cleanse me from all wickedness.

"The third thing, then," Mom B went on, "is by faith to receive Jesus into your heart. Just ask Him to come in and take control of your life."

"You mean that's all there is to it?" I asked.

"That's right. You could say it's as simple as one, two, three!" she replied. "Now let's put those three steps into what we sometimes call the sinner's prayer. Are you ready?"

When I nodded, she asked me to repeat the following prayer after her: "Lord Jesus, I admit I'm a sinner. I ask you to forgive me of all my sins. Right now, by faith, I receive you into my heart. I accept you as my personal Saviour and Lord. Amen."

I glanced up at Mom B. "According to what you just prayed, where is Jesus right now?" she asked.

I thought a moment and replied, "He's in my heart."

She slapped me on the back enthusiastically and said, "That's right, Vicki! Jesus is now in your heart. You see, He doesn't come into a sinful heart. But when we ask Him to forgive our sins, we are washed clean by His blood that He shed for us on the cross. Then we ask Him in. He comes into that cleansed heart. And that's where He is now."

"That's all there is to it?" I asked.

"Well, yes and no. By what you've just prayed, you've

been saved. We also call it 'born again.' But being born again is something like a baby being born into this world. You'll have to grow spiritually, just as a baby grows naturally and physically. You do this by spending time reading and studying the Bible every day. You grow through learning His Word. Begin to share your faith with others. When you do these things, you grow."

Just then Reverend Benton came over. "I saw you two praying over here," he said. "Did anything exciting happen?"

I stood up and smiled. I knew deep down in my heart that somehow I was different, now. Yes, a miracle had happened. I had been born again!

Wigge and Jean saw the excitement and came running. "I've been born again!" I told them.

Wigge threw her arms around me and cried. That was okay. But then I saw Jean's arms heading in my direction. A knot formed in the pit of my stomach. But before I had a chance to do anything, her arms had encircled me. And then another miracle happened. I threw my arms around her! I guess it's up to medical science to decide whether Jean is a man or a woman. But I knew one thing. I was hugging a person—a Christian. And the love that Jesus had just given me was flowing right toward Jean. I couldn't get over it!

We had to go back to our cells, then. But before Mom B left, she told me she would be praying for me. She said God had a great and glorious future for me. That was hard to believe.

Wigge, Jean, and I and a couple of the other girls had some great Bible studies during those next two weeks. The time just seemed to fly by. And then came my day in court.

My first stop there was to see a probation officer. You

know what? One of the first things I spotted on his desk was a Bible!

He introduced himself as Tim Akron and started asking me a bunch of routine questions. But all the time I kept thinking about that Bible. Was he one of us? I had to know.

Finally I blurted out, "Are you a Christian?"

He smiled and replied, "Yes, I am. Why do you ask?"

"Because I am, too. I got saved two weeks ago yesterday."

"Well, praise the Lord! That's great news!"

I looked around nervously. This Mr. Akron certainly was enthusiastic.

Then he said, "Oops! I forgot I'm not in church! But I think this news is wonderful. Tell me that happened."

So I told him about the Bentons and Sheila and the group from her church.

"Now isn't that a coincidence," he remarked. "Sheila Sandburg is a member of the church I attend. In fact, I'm the one who was able to make the arrangements for her to start that weekly service. Now, as a result, you've received Jesus as your personal Saviour. That is absolutely amazing!"

He looked through my records and asked, "Now, what about your future?"

"Well," I responded, "the first thing I'd better do is change my plea to guilty. Then I guess I'll just have to do what Mom B said. I'm just trusting the Lord that He will give me the grace I need to finish my sentence."

"I can't predict what the judge will do," he said, "but I wouldn't resign myself to anything, yet. But whatever the judge decides, I want you to take it as from the Lord. If He wants you as a witness in prison, He'll give you the grace and strength to serve your sentence."

I nodded. Then he said, "Wait here. I've got to hand this report in. Just make yourself at home. You can read my Bible if you want to."

Mr. Akron must have been gone for at least thirty minutes. During that time I even thought of running out of his office. But I realized that trying to escape would be foolish. I had to prove Christ was real in my life and face up to the consequences of my actions.

When he came back, he was a little out of breath. "Vicki," he said, "I've just had a conference with the judge. He sent me to the district attorney's office. I told him all about you and what has happened to you in jail. This judge once sent a girl to the Walter Hoving Home, and he's been very pleased with the reports he's had about her. Now I don't want you to get your hopes up too high, but I think he might be willing to send another girl up there. And I told him I felt you were the kind of girl who could make it okay."

"What? What did you say?"

"I said I'm trying to get you out of jail and up to the Walter Hoving Home—where the Bentons are."

I squealed with joy at that prospect. But could it possibly happen?

Mr. Akron explained that it costs a lot of money to keep people in jail. So when there is a creative alternative—such as the Walter Hoving Home—a judge may go along with it. Since I'd already agreed to plead guilty, perhaps I'd be placed on probation and sent up there.

"Now don't get your hopes too high," he cautioned again. "This is entirely up to the judge. He didn't commit himself to me; he just asked for information. You will have to go before him. If he says twenty years, it'll be twenty years. If he says a year, it'll be a year. And if he says probation, it'll be probation."

My heart beat wildly, and my hands began to tremble with the excitement and the uncertainty. Mr. Akron reached out and placed his hands over mine. "I know, Vicki," he said, "that this is a terrible position for you to be in. But let's pray right now that Christ will give you peace—no matter what happens."

He prayed one of the most beautiful prayers I had ever heard. He just talked to Jesus as though He was right there with us. And I knew He was because I could sense Him, too. The more Mr. Akron prayed, the calmer I felt. By the time he said amen, the peace had come back. I was ready.

A little later I stood before the judge. When he looked down on me, he seemed so awesome and powerful. And I knew he was because he had the power to put me away —maybe for life.

"Vicki Hensley," the judge said after the assistant district attorney had read the charges against me, "I understand you wish to change your plea?"

"Yes, your honor. I wish to plead guilty."

He questioned whether I was doing this of my own free will, or there had been any coercion, or I had been promised any favors. Satisfied that what I was doing was of my own free will, he leaned forward and looked at me. It felt as though he were looking through me. "I understand from Mr. Akron that you want to do right," he said. "The court has made some phone calls and contacted the Walter Hoving Home in New York. Do you think you could go up there and behave yourself?"

"Oh, yes, your honor!"

"Vicki Hensley," the judge said, "on your plea of guilty to these charges, I hereby sentence you to fifteen years in the Lousiana State Prison for Women."

My knees buckled, and I felt as though I was going to faint. Why had he brought up the Walter Hoving Home and then sentenced me to prison? How could he be so cruel, so unfeeling?

Then I heard him command, "Look up here at me."

When I did, I saw he was smiling. "I shall suspend that sentence," he announced, "providing you go to the Walter Hoving Home for one year and behave yourself."

Well, the tears came gushing when I heard that—tears of joy and excitement. God was giving me another chance to do something with my life. I could hardly believe it.

Mr. Akron, his face wreathed in smiles, came over to escort me from the courtroom. The judge called for him to wait, stepped down from the bench, and headed toward us. Had he changed his mind? I had never heard of a judge coming down to talk to a prisoner.

When he got to us, he said, "Vicki, I want to tell you something. My church supports the Walter Hoving Home, so I'm aware of what they're doing up there. I just wanted to tell you, as a friend, that I'll be praying for you."

The judge's smile was so big that I just couldn't help what I did next. Maybe it was some of Mom B's spirit that influenced me. I threw my arms around him and hugged him tightly. Then it hit me: Would I get arrested for doing that? You just don't hug judges! But I guess I didn't have anything to worry about, because the judge put his arms around me and said, "Vicki, you are my daughter in Christ. I love you as I love my own children. And I have a feeling that you are going to make it—all the way with Christ!"

All my life I had felt as if nobody cared. Now I was finding out differently.

The judge pushed me back a little way and looked into

my eyes. "Just keep your faith in Christ," he told me. "Continue to grow as a Christian. And someday I'd like to see you back in my courtroom, but this time with another girl you're trying to help."

With so many people showing confidence in me, I didn't want to ever disappoint them. Standing in that courtroom, I made a commitment to the Lord. I told Him I'd be back there—not as a prisoner, but asking the judge to send another girl to the Walter Hoving Home.

When I got back to Mr. Akron's office, Sheila Sandburg was there, waiting to see me. We hugged, and she told me, "Vicki, this is so wonderful, I can hardly believe it. You can thank God for Judge Woodfield. He's one in a million. I was praying he would get your case. He's really for people who try to go straight."

Yes, I was indeed fortunate.

They'd already packed my things at the jail, so I didn't get a chance to go back and tell Wigge and Jean and the others the good news. But I know they heard about it.

I spent the rest of that day and night in Sheila's custody. The next day she put me on an airplane for New York. In hours I was at the Walter Hoving Home in Garrison.

It seemed like a dream come true. As I walked in the front door of the fantastic mansion that is a home for girls, the first person to greet me was Mom B—with a big smile and a big hug. That woman never changes!

My year at the home was one of really growing in the Lord. From eight in the morning until noon we were in classes. They call it a school of Christian growth. They teach you from God's Word how to live a Christian life. And it really works.

In the afternoons they taught us good work habits. The girls work in the office, do the cooking, and work outside.

They even drive the dump truck!

That year flew by. At graduation I felt so proud. I really had grown as a Christian. I would be better able to help others.

Now I'm back in New Orleans. I've joined the large church that Sheila and Tim Akron attend. They have lots of activities for young people, and they also have their own Bible school that meets two nights a week. I'm a student in it because I've found out you can never learn too much about the Bible.

On Sunday afternoons, now, I go to jail—the same jail where I had been held. But now I go to tell the girls there how Jesus can give them freedom—real freedom.

Sheila helped get Wigge out on probation, and Jean got a six-month sentence and is now back home and has joined a church. She keeps Sheila informed of her progress. She went to a Christian counselor and decided she should change her life-style back to that of a man. It's been a difficult adjustment for her, but Christ is giving the needed grace, and every day it is a little easier. Surely Christ can do anything!

And Christ is still doing things in my life. Just a few weeks ago I stood in Judge Woodfield's court on behalf of a girl who had been saved in our services at the prison. Stephanie was a teenage drug addict, but she really wanted to get her life straightened out. And she made good progress in prison while she was waiting for her day in court. I reminded the judge how he had given me a chance by sending me to the Walter Hoving Home instead of to prison— and how I had come back to be a useful citizen in New Orleans. Then I asked him to send Stephanie to the Walter Hoving Home, to give her a chance like I had been given. Well, he agreed. And I really believe she is going to make it. Jesus can do anything!

Well, that's *my* story—so far. But what about *you*?

Do you know Jesus as your Saviour? Maybe you're reading my story in prison. Maybe you're at home. You could be a good person, a bad person, or somewhere in between. Maybe you're even as mixed up as Jean Hockett was. No matter. Christ is the same for all. He wants to give His love to you and heal your broken heart. He wants to make your life worth living.

Maybe you've been hurt deeply in life—even as a child. Maybe you've been misunderstood and rejected. Maybe you feel that your parents really don't want you around. I know what that's like. I've been there. But I also know that the only answer is Jesus Christ.

It's easy to take Him as your Saviour. All you have to do to be born again is to acknowledge that you are a sinner, ask Christ to forgive all your sins, and receive Him by faith as your Saviour. Remember what Mom B told me? It's as easy as one, two, three!

But what comes after that is also important. When you are born again, you are just a babe in Christ. You've got to grow as a Christian. So establish yourself with a Bible-believing church and study the Bible and witness to others about what Jesus has done for you. All those steps will help you grow. And believe me, it works.

Why don't you receive Jesus as your Saviour, right now? What do you have to lose but your sin, your guilt, your fear, your frustration, your anger, your hopelessness? He will give you peace and forgiveness and love.

Take it from me. I've been where you are. And the greatest decision I ever made was to ask Jesus into my heart. In fact, that decision was when my life really started. In Him I've found out what life is all about—Jesus and love!

The Walter Hoving Home.

Some good things are happening at The Walter Hoving Home.

Dramatic and beautiful changes have been taking place in the lives of many girls since the Home began in 1967. Ninety-four percent of the graduates who have come with problems such as narcotic addiction, alcoholism and delinquency have found release and happiness in a new way of living—with Christ. The continued success of this work is made possible through contributions from individuals who are concerned about helping a girl gain freedom from enslaving habits. Will you join with us in this work by sending a check?

The Walter Hoving Home
Box 194
Garrison, New York 10524
(914) 424-3674

Your Gifts Are Tax Deductible